MARIE CURIOUS

GIRL GENIUS

RESCUES
A
ROCK STAR

BY CHRIS EDISON

Special thanks to Adrian Bott for
bringing Marie Curious to life.

With thanks to Inclusive Minds for connecting
us with their Inclusion Ambassador network,
and in particular to Emma Zipfel for their input.

MARiE
URiⒶUS
GiRL GENiUS

ORCHARD BOOKS

First published in Great Britain in 2021 by The Watts Publishing Group

1 3 5 7 9 10 8 6 4 2

A CIP catalogue record for this book
is available from the British Library.

ISBN 978 1 40836 007 1

Printed and bound in Great Britain by Clays Ltd, Elcograf S.p.A.

The paper and board used in this book are made from wood from responsible sources.

Orchard Books
An imprint of
Hachette Children's Group
Part of The Watts Publishing Group Limited
Carmelite House
50 Victoria Embankment
London EC4Y 0DZ

An Hachette UK Company
www.hachette.co.uk
www.hachettechildrens.co.uk

Contents

Prologue

Marie slowly made her way into the gloomy kitchen, her heart pounding like a drum.

A single bare lightbulb lit the room. The sink was piled with dirty plates. Old window boxes were stacked on every surface. The air stank of potting compost and something else – a thick, sweetly sour, tarry smell that made Marie think of the school biology lab. It made her eyes water.

Every surface, every crooked shelf and filthy worktop, was covered with plants. They looked twisted, as if some evil force had corrupted them. Marie saw thorns as long as her thumb, bloated pods, drooping

dark green tendrils.

I'm way out of my depth, she thought. *This guy isn't just an abductor. He's something much worse. I have to be brave,* she told herself. *He's taken my friend and I need to find her.*

One door led back into the dimly lit house. Another looked like it must lead to the conservatory. The muffled sound of pop music came from behind the conservatory door.

Marie quickly tried to think up a plan. "Everyone, get your phones ready. We need to catch him on video so he can't lie his way out of this."

She took a deep breath – and next moment, it burst out of her in a scream. The door was opening. Pale, wet eyes stared into hers.

It was him. He had been here all along, listening. And now he had her, too . . .

Chapter One

It was risky and reckless, but who cared about that? There were some things you just had to do, because the moment called for it and that moment might never come again.

Marie Trelawney made up her mind. She climbed up on to the V-shaped end of the safety rail at the prow of Sterling Vance's yacht, stood there for a wobbly moment, steadied herself and spread her arms wide into the wind. Her long, luxuriant braids streamed in the breeze.

"I'm the king of the world!" she called as they cruised past St Paul's Cathedral and other London landmarks.

"Marie Curious is the kween of the world!"

Her mother had given her the nickname when she was small. Lately, Marie had been living up to it like never before. She wasn't just exploring the world of science but solving mysteries too.

The immense yacht cruised steadily up the Thames, a white and smoked glass monument to the power of money. Its owner, Sterling Vance, had named it the *Ada Lovelace* in honour of the British mathematical genius.

Smaller ships blew their horns in salute. A tour boat packed with sightseers drew close, and people crowded on to one side to see the looming *Ada Lovelace* go past. Marie waved down to them and smiled. Who would have thought that she, once an ordinary schoolgirl, would now be cruising down the Thames in a billionaire's yacht?

The luxury yacht's ultimate destination was the O2

Arena, the biggest venue in all of London. The last time Marie had been there, it had been to see Billie Eilish in concert. Marie thought back to that night, and her school friends chatting excitedly in the taxi. They had danced together all night.

Marie looked down at the water swirling past far below. She couldn't believe how much her life had changed since going to science camp in America last summer.

"Marie! What in the heck do you think you're doing?"

"Whoa!" Marie snapped back into reality. She quickly climbed down from her perch on the safety rail and turned around.

Sterling Vance was advancing on her, dressed in a sharp evening suit of platinum grey that matched his hair and eyes. His face was filled with panic.

"Sorry, Mr Vance," Marie spluttered. "I was just . . . ah

. . . caught up in the moment, you know?"

"Let me remind you of something," Sterling Vance said. "We are here for Vance Expo. Four happy days of showing off VanceCorp's achievements to the world, ending in what?"

Marie looked blank. "Um. A big party?"

"Ending in the launch of the *Solid Sterling* record label!" Vance rolled his eyes. "Sheesh. Yes, the tech stuff is important, but the future of VanceCorp is in music. We're going to take on the world. Now, I need you to stay focused. You falling into the river is not a good way to launch my label!"

Marie leaned against the rail and tried to look unruffled. "I didn't fall in," she protested.

"But you could have, Marie." Vance glanced down into the churning foam. "What kind of publicity would that have been? There are millions of dollars at stake!

I have some big surprises lined up for the press, and you drowning isn't one of them!"

Marie had almost forgotten about Vance's new record label. He was going to take on the world with a combination of new and established artists, with the power of his computer systems backing them up. If Marie hadn't been one of Vance's four apprentices, she wouldn't have been brought along.

Anyway, apprentice or not, she could look after herself. She straightened her shoulders and narrowed her eyes.

"Since when did you dream of being a music mogul, Mr Vance?" she said boldly. "You told us you'd wanted to be an inventor ever since you were little!"

"Mutate and survive," Vance said. "If a corporation wants to grow and prosper in an uncertain world, it has to move into new areas. Besides, I've always planned

to get more into music, when the time was right." He reached into his pocket, took out a pair of sunglasses made to look like pixel art, and strolled off.

Marie watched him go. It wasn't really surprising that Vance was worried about his reputation right now. He was still antsy from his near miss with Black Rose. If it hadn't been for Marie and her friends Gabby, Sophie and Elisha, his own company, VanceCorp, might have unleashed a devastating computer virus into the world.

The four girls had been taking part in Vance Camp last summer, a science camp for kids who had a gift for STEM subjects. They had had to act quickly and bravely to thwart the evil engineer who'd come up with the virus, and Vance had been pretty useless in the face of it. Making them all his apprentices had been his way of paying them back.

The friends had won Vance's robotics competition by

inventing astonishing little ant-like robots called GEMS, named after the initials of each of their first names – Gabby, Elisha, Marie, Sophie. Now, after a few months apart, they had been reunited to show off the GEMS they invented – not that Vance hadn't tried to take the lion's share of the credit for coming up with them.

Oh well, Marie thought. At least she had lots of other amazing exhibits at Vance Expo to look forward to. No doubt Vance's record label was just his latest obsession, and he'd go back to science when he got bored of it. Heaven only knew what Vance's idea of good music was, anyway. Probably something like her dad's cheesy rock compilations.

The evening air was starting to get chilly. Marie headed back inside to the yacht's Starlight Lounge, an enormous bar and dance floor area that looked out over the deck. Right now it was almost empty, but Gabby,

Sophie and Elisha were all sat huddled around one table with amazed expressions. Light shone up into their faces from Gabby's laptop.

"Oh my God, Marie, come look at this! It's *incredible!*" Sophie called.

The Australian girl wasn't the kind to hide her enthusiasm, and Marie had grown used to her habit of overblowing things, so she wasn't expecting much. But then Marie saw that Gabby was wide-eyed too, and even Elisha was squealing. Elisha was usually very quiet around other people, except where maths and football were concerned.

This was serious. Marie picked up speed and ran to join them. "What is it? What's going on?"

Gabby pointed with one long acrylic nail. "Look who Vance has booked!"

Her laptop screen showed an announcement that

had just gone live on the VanceCorp website:

BREAKING NEWS!

Sterling Vance, in association with Solid Sterling

Records, is proud to present

CALLIE SUNNY

FOR THE FIRST TIME EVER

LIVE in concert at Vance Expo at the O2 Arena

November 12th

Prior to her upcoming WORLD TOUR

Tickets strictly limited to 20,000 – book now to avoid

disappointment

Beneath the announcement was a photo of a slender girl with dark eyes and bright blue and white twists, sticking her tongue out and making a peace sign.

Marie's head span. She sat down heavily next to

Sophie. *Thank goodness I wasn't balancing on the rail when I heard this news,* she thought. *I might really have fallen in.*

"Callie freakin' Sunny!" Gabby crowed. "How'd he land an act that cool? And a live gig, too? Guess old Vancito is serious about this record label of his."

"No wonder he told me he had millions tied up in this," Marie breathed. "Now we know what he spent them on. Well, who."

Sophie threw one arm around Marie and the other around Gabby. "We'll get to go, right? For free?"

"We'll probably even get to go backstage," Elisha said.

Marie was still struggling to process the news. The four of them all loved Callie Sunny's music. They'd listened to it back at Vance Camp when they were studying together. When they worked through the long night to build the GEMS, the music had helped give them

strength to carry on. Marie hadn't stopped listening to her music since coming back from camp. She loved seeing another black girl smashing it in her industry.

Callie was a massive deal on social media. She blended two of the biggest YouTube interests – music and make-up – and rarely appeared the same way twice, making her own custom costumes for each song. Record-breaking numbers of TikTokers invented dances to samples from songs of hers like *My Friends Call Me Medusa* and *Girls in Crowns.*

And she'd never once done a live show. Until now.

What Marie didn't understand was how Vance had picked her as his main star. Callie Sunny was huge on the internet, and lots of teenagers and people of Marie's age were fans, but many adults hadn't even heard of her.

"So which of you gave Vance the idea?" she joked. "He couldn't have come up with it himself."

Sophie shrugged. "Maybe he has better taste in music than we thought?"

"Nah, it won't be that," Gabby said. "I'll tell you why Vance chose her. It's because Callie Sunny is a self-starter, y'know? Worked her way up from nothing. Did it all her own way. That's the kind of person Vance likes."

Elisha sat suddenly upright. "Wait. Can anyone else hear that?"

From outside, getting louder by the moment, came the unmistakable sound of thousands of people cheering.

Chapter Two

Marie and the other girls raced out on to the deck. The gigantic dome of the O2 Arena loomed up to their left. They were almost there! And for some reason, there was a massive crowd gathered all along North Greenwich Pier. They whooped and cheered as the *Ada Lovelace* drew steadily closer.

"I guess they're all hoping to catch a glimpse of Sterling Vance," Marie said.

"Or maybe Callie Sunny," added Sophie.

The enormous yacht glided to a stop. With a soft hum, walkways with handrails unfolded from the side and clamped themselves to the pier. More and more

VanceCorp employees were coming up on deck now, but they weren't leaving the yacht. They seemed to be waiting for something.

A man in dark glasses and a black suit muttered something into his headset, nodded, and went over to Marie.

"Mr Vance would like you to go and meet the fans with him," he said. He gestured to the pier.

Marie, Elisha and Sophie looked at one another in astonishment. Gabby wore a sly grin.

"He wants US to meet them?" said Elisha in something rather like horror.

"But he's the famous one, not us!" Marie burst out.

"Why do I have a bad feeling about this . . . ?" said Sophie hollowly.

"Over here, girls," called Vance, clicking his fingers. "Let's go introduce you to the world."

As Vance stepped from the boat on to the pier with the girls following close behind, the fans crowded around them. Happy, wide-eyed faces stared into theirs.

"Hey!" yelled a skinny boy in glasses, waving frantically at Marie. "Have you been signed to Solid Sterling?"

"I'm not a pop star," Marie answered immediately. "I'm something way cooler – a scientist."

The crowd clapped and laughed.

"These are my four apprentices – Gabby, Elisha, Marie and Sophie," said Vance, beaming. "Educational opportunities like this are just one of the many ways VanceCorp gives back to the community and supports women in STEM. I'm so delighted to be teaching these girls everything I know."

Marie rolled her eyes. Sterling Vance was a clever businessman, but he wasn't the talented inventor the world thought he was.

"What's it like working with the genius who created the GEMS?" asked another fan.

Vance grinned. "They're still pretty star-struck, but they're getting used to it."

"Excuse me? *We* invented them, not you!" Marie snapped.

"Just smile and wave, and leave the questions to me," Vance told her with a wink.

Marie tried to push forwards through the throng, but it wasn't easy. The feeling of so many strange bodies pressing against her was like riding the tube during rush hour, only worse. "Excuse me," she said politely. It made no difference.

The questions kept coming. "What do your parents think about your apprenticeship?" "What inventions are you working on now?" "What's the most important thing Vance has taught you?"

"How *not* to launch a software update!" Sophie huffed. Beside her, Elisha pulled her jacket over her head and ran forwards.

To Marie's relief, she spotted a long silver limousine on the far side of the ferry terminal bridge. "That's our ride. Come on!"

The four girls hurried towards the waiting limousine. Vance jogged along and caught up. Just as he was reaching for the door handle, a startling young woman appeared from behind the car. She was short and bright-eyed, with curly bright-blonde hair and a polka-dot ensemble.

I've seen this person before, Marie thought.

"Hello, hello! Glad I could catch you!" The woman smiled in a way that made Marie think of plastic shop mannequins. She shook Vance's hand. "I'm Hayley MacKenzie. Nice to meet you."

"Of course!" Marie said. "The live streamer. I've seen your videos!"

"Can we get in the car, please?" said Elisha.

"Just a sec," said Hayley. "We need to talk biz. Mr Vance, would you do me the honour of appearing on my show?"

Vance sighed. "Sorry, Hayley. I'd love to, but my schedule's packed. But why don't these four take my place? They've always got lots to talk about."

Hayley glanced at the girls in disappointment. "If you're really not available, Mr Vance, then . . . sure, why don't you four come to my studio the day after tomorrow? I'll email with all the deets. Ta-ta for now!"

With that, Hayley hopped on to a scooter and zoomed away, leaving the girls stunned.

"What just happened?" Marie said.

Gabby facepalmed. "We just got booked to go on a

livestream show!"

"Oops," said Sophie.

Elisha leaned against the side of the car to steady herself. "What even *is* her show?"

"The Anti-Boredom Agenda?" Marie said. "It's all sorts, really. They make new types of slime, test out the latest gadgets, rank the best fail compilations of the week, that kind of thing. They've got, like, millions of subscribers. Mostly kids. It could be a good way to get more girls interested in science."

Elisha groaned. Sophie hugged her. "Don't worry. We don't have to go through with it."

Vance held up a warning hand. "Whoa. You're my apprentices. I need you to go and represent VanceCorp on Hayley's show. You need new clothes or whatever for the occasion, fine. Tap the expense account. But you are not backing out."

The limousine dropped Vance and his apprentices off at his luxurious hotel, where everybody had a five-course dinner. The table was heaped with dishes like lobster and veal, which Sophie refused to touch. Gabby finally got to try caviar, seconds before spitting it out in a potted plant. "Like salted boogers," she explained with a grimace.

After that, a taxi took the four girls to North London where Marie lived.

Marie's palms were sweaty as she sat on the back seat. This was the part of today she'd been dreading the most.

All of the VanceCorp team were staying at the same hotel, and at first Vance had assumed the girls would be, too. But Marie had had other plans.

"Come and stay at my house!" she'd told them.

"You can meet my mum and Izzy my cat, and see my Inventing Shed, and we can stay up late and watch anime and make s'mores . . ."

"Or you can enjoy an entire hotel suite, with unlimited personal expenses. Each," Vance had said. "Your call."

Marie had relished the look on Vance's face when all the girls had accepted her offer instead of his.

That happy moment seemed very far away now. What would her friends make of her life? She hadn't told them very much about her mum's illness. Sometimes people treated her mum like she must be completely helpless, just because she used a wheelchair. That was horrible. Then there were the people who tried to pretend the wheelchair wasn't really there, like it was some kind of guilty secret. That was almost worse.

But on top of that, her mum had a habit of saying

exactly what she thought about other people and their life choices. It had led to some major drama in the past. *Please*, Marie prayed, don't let any of them upset her ... or her them ...

Gabby yawned. "What time is it? I'm beat."

"Almost eleven," said Sophie. "I've been awake for about twenty-four hours now. Sydney to London. I'm exhausted!"

"I'm not surprised. You skipped an entire night's sleep!" Marie said, thankful that she'd only had to take the tube to meet Vance and her friends instead of flying halfway around the world like they had.

"Jet lag," groaned Elisha. "It's 3.30 am in New Delhi. The time difference is killing me!"

"I'm wide awake," chimed Gabby. "New York is five hours behind London. It's only the afternoon for me."

The limousine pulled up outside Marie's modest

terraced house. She looked at it, embarrassed. The front garden was overgrown because neither she nor her mum had bothered to mow it since she'd come back from camp, and the purple paint on the front door was a bit chipped. *I hope they think it's OK,* she thought.

The driver fetched their bags while Marie unlocked the door and let them in.

"Mum?" she called softly.

"Welcome to London!" came the response.

Dina was in the hallway waiting. She was wearing a big smile on her face and had decorated the hall with a WELCOME sign for Marie's friends.

"It's so nice to finally meet you all," said Dina to Sophie, Elisha and Gabby. "Marie has told me so much about you that I already feel like I know you all really well."

Marie rolled her eyes, embarrassed by her mum's over-the-top welcome. "Why don't we go in to the living

room," she said, motioning for the girls to follow.

As Marie led the girls through to the living room she stopped in her tracks. The dining table was against the wall. So were the chairs. The floor had been turned into a sleepover space, with inflatable mattresses, sleeping bags and cushions for all four of them. Marie's mum couldn't have done all this without Kate, her nurse, helping out. Marie recognised some of the covers and quilts from the very depths of the airing cupboard. Was that the princess sleeping bag she'd had when she was *eight*?

She thought about the five-star hotel the girls had turned down so they could be here, and cringed.

"Welcome to the Casa del Trelawney," she said, turning to them with an apologetic grin. But the girls were already piling into the room, giggling happily.

"This looks so cool. Thank you, Mrs Trelawney!"

said Elisha, putting her bag down.

"Sleep-o-ver!" Sophie chanted. "Sleep-o-ver!" She picked up a lavender pillow with frilly edges that had belonged to Marie's grandmother, and bopped Elisha on the head with it. Elisha laughed and backed away into the kitchen.

"Hey, keep it down, you two!" Gabby hissed. "Marie has neighbours!"

"Oh, sorry!" Sophie unzipped her pack and began to pull her belongings out. She held up a yellow toothbrush. "Where's your dunny, Marie?"

"We mostly just use the downstairs one . . . it's through at the back of the kitchen. Guys, are you sure this is OK?" said Marie.

Gabby looked blank. "What do you mean?"

"You don't want to head to the hotel instead? This is all a bit basic. I know you wanted to take lots of pictures

33

for your Instas, and this isn't exactly Insta worthy." She held up a twill, lilac pillow.

Gabby shook her head, tutted and gave Marie a sudden tight hug. After a moment, she pulled away and looked Marie right in the eye. "*Chica*, you worry way too much. Look at this cool camp your mama's made for us! It will be so much fun!"

Not long after, Marie lay under the table on a blow-up air bed, snuggled up in a sleeping bag and with Izzy curled up in the crook of her arm. Her three best friends lay nearby, fast asleep and in Sophie's case, gently snoring.

She felt her eyelids drooping, and her last thought before sleep took her was: *Tomorrow is going to be a MASSIVE day* . . .

Chapter Three

The blurry light shining in between the table legs told Marie it was morning. There was a thick, sweet, smell in the air that reminded her of the school holidays, and animated conversation in her ears. She grimaced, rubbed her eyes and looked out over the floor. She saw only carpet. All the other girls' bedding had been tidied neatly away. Two thoughts came into her head, hard on each other's heels:

Mum's making pancakes!

. . . wait, am I the last one up?

"Mum?" she called.

"What kind of time do you call this to be getting up?"

came the merry response. "Come and eat something before it all goes cold!"

Marie bounded out of the sleeping bag and charged through to the kitchen. Her mother was sitting at the little kitchen table, with Elisha, Gabby and Sophie.

As Marie started on her breakfast pancakes, the other girls chatted to her mum. They all seemed to be hitting it off fantastically. Marie felt her anxiety melting away like the chocolate chips in her pancakes. This wasn't awkward. In fact, it was just as if they'd all known one another for years.

After breakfast, while Elisha sat on the sofa and worked on a Sudoku puzzle with Dina, and Sophie washed up the plates, Gabby started a complete overhaul of the household internet. "Who puts their router at the back of the house, on top of the microwave?" she said in exasperation. "Marie, was this you?"

"It's kind of always been there?" Marie said with a hopeless shrug.

"Oh, honey. We can do so much better than this. Come on. We're going shopping."

"Shopping" turned out to mean selecting an assortment of Vance gadgets online – one of the perks of their apprenticeship. By the time midday rolled around, a brand-new router had been set up in a central location and everyone was getting stacks of bandwidth wherever they went in the house. Gabby had installed apps on Dina's phone to control the lighting, the thermostat and even a security camera on the front door.

"I'm queen of the castle!" Dina laughed. "So tell me, girls, what hasn't my daughter told me about what she got up to in America last summer? Did she meet someone special? Come on. I want all the gossip she's been hiding from me."

To Marie's immense relief, that was when her phone rang. "It's Dad! He's Facetiming me!"

She held her phone up and everyone crowded around to watch. Her dad's image appeared, crisp and clear, thanks to the newly boosted internet. He was sitting behind his desk in a cramped little office on the oil rig where he worked.

"What's this?" he laughed as he saw all the faces. "The Spanish Inquisition?"

"I've finally met Marie's friends from camp!" Dina called.

Marie introduced the girls to her dad and launched into an excited babbling description of Vance Expo. "We'll be showing off the ant robots we made, and there's a music label too, and oh God, Callie Sunny's going to be there, she's this rock star, and we've got to go on a YouTube show, and and and . . ."

"Steady on," her dad said, holding his hands up. "One thing at a time, love."

As Marie chatted to her father, she felt the last of her tension disappear. For this brief moment, the people she loved the most were all together. *I have to remember this feeling,* she thought. *This unity. The next few days might be full on, but y'know ... I think I can handle them.*

After lunch, Marie took the girls through to her Inventing Shed. The girls marvelled at her poster collection and the inventions she'd assembled over the years. Then it was time to get to work.

Marie took out a little ant-like robot, one of the GEMS they'd invented together, and set it on her workbench. "We're meant to be showing these off tomorrow at

Vance Expo," she said. "If there's one thing that gets people excited, it's an upgrade. So how can we make these GEMS even better?"

They spent the next half hour brainstorming ideas and settling on their chosen projects. Elisha decided on liquid crystal plating, so the GEMS could change their appearance to blend in with their background. Marie opted to give them swappable tool arms for different jobs – "like doll accessories" as Gabby helpfully put it. Sophie suggested a solar-powered charging unit, and Gabby a magnetic rotor-pack that could be clipped on to a GEM to allow it to hover like a drone. They couldn't build the finished designs with the equipment Marie had in her shed, but they could definitely make mock-ups as a proof of concept, and that was plenty to be going on with.

As they worked, Marie's cat Izzy sauntered into the

shed. He settled on Marie's lap and allowed her to make a fuss of him for a moment, then suddenly changed his mind and strutted off to curl up on Elisha's lap instead.

"Thanks, Iz," Marie laughed.

Elisha rubbed Izzy under his chin, and he stretched his face forwards with his eyes closed in bliss. Marie was impressed. "He likes you."

As they worked through the afternoon, Izzy took turns sitting on each of them, as if he was carrying out an experiment of his own. He returned to Marie's lap in the end, to her private satisfaction.

"He knows who feeds him!" Sophie said, laughing.

"Bedtime!" came the call from the house.

"What? No way." Marie glanced out the window and saw it was pitch dark outside. "Guys, what time is it?"

"It's nine already," Gabby said. "We must have been really into it. The day went by like *that*." She snapped

her fingers together.

"Girls! Bed! You have a big day tomorrow!" Dina called, more firmly this time.

As they headed back into the house, Marie's phone buzzed. A Insta notification? She checked and saw Hayley McKenzie had tagged her in a post about her upcoming show.

My guest @Curious_Marie42 has engineering in her blood. Dad's an oil engineer, and Marie herself is apprenticed to the one and only Sterling Vance! We'll be asking: what really makes this tech girl tick? Find out soon on #AntiBoredomAgenda!

Marie's stomach lurched. She told herself: it's nothing bad, stay calm, it's all just promotion. But the sense of being thrust into the spotlight was back with a vengeance. She hadn't told Hayley about her dad's job. That meant the bubbly little blogger had been doing

her own research on Marie. The thought that someone had been digging into her life made her skin crawl.

She was glad Gabby had put a security camera on the front door ...

Chapter Four

"Welcome to Vance Expo," smiled the woman at the reception desk. "Are you here on a school trip?"

"Oh, no," said Marie, handing over her identity card. "We're exhibitors. With VanceCorp."

She enjoyed the look of surprise on the woman's face. Without a word, she made up lanyards for them all with laminated passes on the end. They hung them around their necks as if they were prize medals.

The huge dome of the O2 Arena had been specially converted into an exhibition space. Today was for press and VIPs only, not the general public. The ground floor was a warren of demonstration stands, podiums with

futuristic vehicles on, booths, back-to-back cubicles and coffee tables. High above it all hung a suspended dining pod with corkscrew metal stairs winding up to it – the Executive Lounge, going by the signs. It looked like a silver UFO.

Sophie opened up the glossy programme and found a map. "Our booth's this way. Let's go get set up."

"Do we have to run the stall all day? I want to explore while it's nice and quiet," Elisha said, looking longingly at a rotating molecule sculpture.

"Why don't we take it in shifts?" suggested Marie.

Everyone agreed this was a brilliant plan. Two of the girls would stay and show off the GEMS to any journalist who visited their stall, while the other two went off and enjoyed the Expo. Then they'd change roles every hour.

Their booth was a corner unit with a large sign at the top reading *GEMS!* in colour-changing holographic

foil, along with photos of all four of them. There was an L-shaped counter for the girls to stand at, which on closer inspection turned out to be a glass-topped display case rather like a scaled-up ant farm, for the GEMS to scuttle around in. There were sections where the little bots could operate miniature machines, pull each other around on trolleys, and move sand and blocks around to build constructions. The girls had designed it themselves, and Vance had had it brought perfectly to life.

Marie and Elisha took the first shift. They smiled politely at the journalists who passed by their booth, but only a few showed any interest. One of them muttered something about a "school science fair" as he wandered off, which made Marie's blood boil.

"Like to see *you* program a hive mind," Marie said under her breath.

Sophie and Gabby soon came racing back, breathless and bright-eyed. Sophie was covered with grey hairs. "I got to cuddle a *wolf!*" she burst out. "A real live one!"

"Who brought wolves to a tech show?" Elisha asked.

"It's a genetics company. They're working on animal cloning to save species from extinction. And Gabby nearly got headhunted!"

Gabby admired her nails. "I said no, of course. But when you're so good at hacking that a cyber security company wants to hire you to test out their systems, you gotta take the compliment."

Marie and Elisha headed out to explore. Elisha immediately stopped at a booth offering a full-body virtual reality adventure – not just a helmet, but a pad that moved under your feet as you ran. "I've got to try this," she said. In moments she was sprinting through a digital jungle, sliding under flaming log traps and

kicking flying skulls at giant demon apes.

"You might want to turn up the difficulty a bit," Marie told the booth operator.

He made a note. "It doesn't go up any higher," he admitted. "But I can see now that it needs to . . ."

Marie left them to it and headed off through the stalls. Most of them were run by different divisions of VanceCorp, offering amazing new devices. A home music system could scan your brain and decide what tracks you most needed to hear at that moment, to calm you down or fire you up. New VR games used lasers to beam digital images right inside your eyes. Marie lingered at the space exploration exhibit, which was showing a model of the planned Vance orbital station, and gave the military exhibit a wide berth.

Strange, she thought. Vance made such a big deal of his record label, but I can't see any sign of it. I wonder

where the booth for that is?

Next second, as she emerged from the end of the exhibition area, she had her answer. A tall black stage was being prepped, complete with speakers that would dwarf Stonehenge. The lighting rig was half assembled. This must all be for the big concert at the end of the week.

Marie suddenly felt more excited than ever. Callie Sunny, here in person! And only a few days to go until the concert!

She strolled up to the stage, imagining the arena filled with cheering fans and herself right at the front. Who could have foreseen all of this a month ago? Life truly was serving up some curveballs.

She spent the rest of the hour wandering around in a blissful daze. She began to get a funny, slightly creepy feeling, and next moment she noticed that a

pale woman standing in the Vance Robotics booth was staring at her. She had startling blue eyes.

Marie headed over. "Is something wrong?" she said boldly.

"Hello," said the woman in a halting voice. "How are you? My name is Esther. I am one day old today. I am a Vance android."

Marie's mouth fell open. A real android – her first ever! "Pleased to meet you, Esther," she said, wondering if robots understood manners.

Esther smiled, but a little too slowly, so what should have been a friendly smile turned into a strange leer. They obviously hadn't got the programming quite right yet! Marie's creepy feeling went up a few notches, but she wanted to find out more about Esther and her mechanics. She asked her lots of questions about her programming and her processing speed whilst

examining Esther's life-like features.

Eventually she asked the question she had always wanted to ask an android. "Are you happy?"

Esther blinked with a click of her eyelids. "Of course I am happy. I was created to be happy. How could I be anything else?"

Marie returned to the GEMS booth, where the other girls were looking as frazzled as she felt. "I don't know about any of you, but I could use a lunch break," Marie said.

"Good call," said Gabby. "There's a coffee bar thing just over there."

"Why settle for that, when we could chill out in style?" Sophie said. She pointed up above their heads to the circular Executive Lounge, hanging in its cradle of metal struts and cables.

"Are we even allowed up there?" Marie wondered.

Gabby brandished her lanyard. "Of course! We're Vance's apprentices, aren't we? We can go anywhere!"

Not feeling entirely certain of that, Marie climbed up the creaking metal staircase with her friends. Inside, the place was like a millionaire YouTuber's mansion. All the sofas were plush, vending machines offered customized pizzas in all imaginable varieties, glass tubes of neon-coloured sweets poured their contents into hand-held baskets and tinted windows looked out over the exhibition hall below.

Most of the seats were already taken. At some, reporters with press badges typed on laptops. At the others, huddles of corporate types in expensive clothes sat drinking champagne. They looked disdainfully at the girls as they entered.

"Hi!" Gabby said loudly into their faces. "How are all you guys doin'?"

"There's the food," Marie said, and hurried towards the restaurant area. Soon after, with arms full of freshly made milkshakes, chips and toasted paninis, they edged back between the tables, trying to find somewhere free to sit. Wherever they looked, adults frowned at them, tutted or whispered behind their hands.

"Bet they wouldn't be giving us this attitude if Vance was here," said Sophie irritably.

"Yeah," said Elisha. "He has his uses."

Marie looked towards the other side of the lounge, directly overlooking the exhibition space, where some sort of presentation was being set up. A young girl wearing a blue technician's cap and safety goggles was standing on a platform, fiddling with a set of keyboards and speakers.

She caught Marie's eye and grinned. Marie guessed she was a sound technician, judging by the tools poking

out of her pocket and the headphones around her neck.

"Hey, would you mind doing me a favour?" the girl said in a Californian accent.

"Sure," said Marie, leading the others to an empty table nearby.

"You know a USB from a HDMI, right?"

"Well, duh!"

"Cool. I've got to get a lot of cables in place and I haven't got long to do it. Could you hook the speaker over there to the mixing desk?"

"I love a challenge," Marie replied. "Let's go."

Using her foot, the girl slid a Tupperware box of tangled cables over to Marie, who set to work immediately. Gabby downed her milkshake and came over to help.

"What do we call you?" Gabby asked the girl.

She cocked her head and looked pensive. "You can

call me Sparks," she said.

Sparks bent over the synthesiser, flicking switches and adjusting the sound balance. She was so confident in what she was doing. Marie was impressed. "You must have been doing this for some time," she said.

"Quite a few years," said Sparks. "Hey, Gabby, would you pass that screwdriver?"

"Sure," Gabby said. She held out the screwdriver and then did the first real-life double take that Marie had ever seen. "Wait, WHAT?"

"Thanks," Sparks said, a grin on her face.

Marie looked at Gabby. "What's wrong?"

"I didn't tell her my name!" Gabby said.

"She's right, Marie," said Sparks, adjusting a screw. "She didn't."

Marie paused and stared. Her head seemed to be spinning gently around, or maybe it was the room.

"How do you know who we are?"

"Come on, are you kidding? You four are legends!" Sparks tossed the screwdriver in the air, caught it and tucked it away. "I was watching the livestream when you guys saved the day at Vance HQ. If you hadn't have come up here first, I was going to go visit your booth and say hi. I'm a bit of a science nerd myself. That's why I agreed to work this tech fair."

Marie laughed. Somehow, Sparks didn't seem as scary as the mass of fans on the pier, or as daunting as Hayley Mackenzie.

Marie finished connecting up the amp and stepped away. "All done. So, who's performing today? There was no one mentioned in the programme."

"This wasn't on the programme," Sparks said. "There's going to be a private mini-gig for the first-day attendees. By Callie Sunny."

"Seriously?" Marie gawped.

Gabby squealed. "Oh, we love her!"

"Ehh," said Sparks and wrinkled her nose. "I think her voice is kind of annoying." She put her headphones on and began twisting knobs.

Marie and Gabby glanced at one another. How could anyone not love Callie Sunny?

Just then, a tall, well-built woman in a sharp suit and sunglasses came briskly over to their table. Her hair was raven black and cut very short.

She rapped with her knuckles on the girls' table and snapped, "Excuse me, what publication are you with? *Teenzy Trax* or some such nonsense?"

"Um, we're not with any publication," said Marie.

"Oh? Then are you even authorised to attend this concert?" She folded her arms and glared. Before anyone could speak, she said, "Huh. Didn't think so."

"But—" Marie started to say, but the woman gestured for her to stand up.

She said, "Nice try, sweetheart, but I know fans will try anything to get into a Callie Sunny concert. Are you going to leave quietly or am I going to have to use force?"

"Whoa, wait!" Gabby said. "You're with Sterling Vance, right? His security staff know us. If you could just—"

"My name is Rosa Ivanovich," the woman said, "and I am not merely 'with Sterling Vance'. I am Callie Sunny's personal bodyguard. Out."

"But we are with VanceCorps!" Marie protested. She held up her laminated pass for Rosa to read.

Rosa sneered. "Those are merely *exhibitor* passes, not access-all-areas. I see you are determined to be difficult. Do you know what this is?"

Marie felt a cold jolt of fear as Rosa reached into her

jacket. She brought out something that looked like a cross between a barcode scanner and a stapler. It was black, with little prongs sticking out of the barrel and a glowing blue light on its side.

"This is called a stinger," Rose said in a voice of ice. "Like a police taser, but not so gentle. It delivers a jolt of electricity. It will not kill you, but it will knock you out," she said with a grin.

"Let's get out of here," Elisha said.

The girls had no choice but to get up and head for the exit in front of everyone. Journalists looked up at them and sniggered. But then a voice from behind said, "Wait."

It was Sparks, with her headphones off. She tapped Rosa on the shoulder and held up a tablet. "You might want to check the guest list."

"Why?"

"Because their names are on it. See those names at

the bottom? That's these four."

Rosa looked at the names, glanced at the four girls and grunted in disgust. "Why didn't you just *say* you were on the guest list? You like wasting people's time, do you?" She stomped away to guard the stairs, grousing to herself all the way.

The girls sat back down again, feeling confused. Marie looked at the tablet. Sure enough, their names were there.

Sparks met Marie's eye, gave her a sly wink and turned back to her keyboards.

"She must have edited the list on the spot!" Marie whispered.

"Dang, she's good," Gabby said approvingly.

Behind them, the lounge was quickly filling up. People crowded amongst the tables, unable to find seats. Marie fidgeted with excitement. She'd never been on

the guest list for a concert before. Well, except her uncle Eric's soul and funk tribute band, Fool and the Gang, and they were pretty terrible.

"I can't believe Callie Sunny's going to be here any moment!" whispered Sophie.

"Oh my God, guys," Marie said. "Look."

Up on the stage, a transformation was taking place. Sparks the sound engineer took off her goggles and her cap, and shook out her long bright blue and white twists. She unzipped her technician's vest, revealing a tatty white T-shirt covered in graffiti designs.

The girls sat in speechless amazement.

Eventually, Elisha said, "I knew she was a chameleon, but I never thought I'd see it up close like this."

Marie couldn't believe her eyes. "Call me Sparks," the girl had said, but now Marie realised that wasn't her real name at all.

The girl in front of her now – the friendly, tech-savvy girl who knew Marie's name and had called her a legend – wasn't Callie Sunny's sound technician.

She was Callie Sunny!

Chapter Five

"Hi, folks," Callie said into the microphone. "My name's Callie Sunny, and I'm so excited about signing up with Solid Sterling. If you've heard my old stuff, thank you for sticking with me. If you haven't, I guess you could always ask your kids who I am."

Polite laughter rippled around the room. Marie's stomach tightened in a knot. She felt the strangest urge to protect Callie from the people here. They didn't *get* her at all. The singer looked completely out of her element, like that time when Izzy had to be taken to the vet in a cat carrier and was suddenly surrounded by dogs. *Poor thing,* she'd thought; he's been used to being

the swaggering king of his own domain and now he's just a frightened moggy.

Don't be stupid, she told herself. *This is Callie Sunny. She's a professional.*

"This is the headliner from my new album," Callie said. "Hope you like it. It's called *Blue Summer Skies.*"

She pressed a button and a jaunty dance beat started up. Callie's fingers danced across the keyboard. Rainbow lighting flickered across Rosa's stern face. Callie sang:

Blue summer skies lighting up my brain.

No more heartache and no more pain.

Just can't wait until I see you again.

Oooh . . .

Marie wasn't sure what to make of it at all. What had happened to Callie's signature electropop sound? She normally sang songs about getting to know the monsters in your head and having anxiety in gym

class. These lyrics were telling a story about going off to summer camp and meeting a special someone. It was unbelievably upbeat, positive stuff, more like what you'd get from a manufactured girl band than a solo singer-songwriter.

The audience were lapping it up, though. When Callie had finished, they all got up and gave her a standing ovation.

"That's all for now," Callie said softly. "You want to ask me anything, go ahead."

"Just one song?" Sophie said to Marie. "Short gig."

The people in the room began to surge forward to talk to her, pushing past Marie and the other girls, but Rosa strode forward. "Three at a time only!" she barked. "You, you and you. Come. The rest, form a line!"

"So what did you think?" Elisha whispered.

"Um. It was OK, I guess?" Marie said. "I kind of wanted

to hear more of her old stuff."

"Me too," Gabby said, with a look of relief. "I mean, I'd dance to it? But it wouldn't make my top three."

"Or my top five," Marie said.

"Guys, c'mon," Sophie insisted. "We're the first people in the *world* to hear a new Callie song. There're people who'd give their kidneys to be here!"

Eventually, the flood of journalists died down. Rosa was making sure none of them spoke to Callie for more than their allowed time. A tabloid photographer was being too pushy until Rosa offered to throw him down the stairs. He laughed, as if she was joking, but the laughter died away as she reached for the stinger. "Try me," she said.

"Well, Callie's not going to want to hang around with us. Shall we get back to the booth?" Marie said.

"Yeah." Gabby glanced at Callie. "Too bad. She's nice."

But just as they were about to leave, they heard Callie call them. They walked over with Rosa's watchful eye on them at all times. She was like Callie's personal guard dog.

"Sorry about pranking you before, but I couldn't resist," Callie grinned.

"I can't believe we didn't recognise you!" Marie said in disbelief.

Callie laughed. "I love dressing up. Changing my face, trying on new looks. When I was little I wanted to be a spy. My dad and I used to play secret agents."

They sat together and chatted for a while like old friends. When Callie asked what they'd thought of the new song, all the girls told her how much they'd liked it. Callie smiled, but Marie noticed the smile didn't reach her eyes. For some reason she thought of Esther the android's robotic smile.

"So, what are you guys up to later?" Callie eventually said, taking a gulp of mineral water.

"Er, nothing?" Marie shrugged.

Callie spread her fingers and turned her face to the sky. "Oh, thank God. I need people my age to talk to or I swear I'll do something crazy. I am surrounded by adults *all* the time. It's like prison."

Her phone buzzed. She took her it out and Marie saw the case was covered with little blue gems. She checked a message, scowled and put it away again. "How would you all like to come to an exclusive all-star rooftop party this evening? Same hotel as Mr Vance and all his staff."

The girls looked at one another with shock that rapidly turned into delight. But before they could say anything, Rosa stepped in, stony-faced.

"I do not think this is such a good idea," she said. "You

want to invite total strangers to party with you, with everything that's been happening recently?"

"I'm sure it will be fine, Rosa," Callie insisted. "Well? Can you come?"

"I don't know," Elisha said. "Parties aren't really my thing. No offence, I'm just—"

"Of course we'll come," Gabby said, grabbing Callie's hand in hers. "Ohmygodohmygod. Thank you. You're amazing!"

Back in Marie's living room, the dining table was piled high with sparkly eyeshadows, hair clips, bracelets, and the girls' most glam clothes. They had pooled their resources and even raided Marie's mum's wardrobe for some vintage pieces, much to Dina's amusement. They

were in full makeover mode.

Marie paced up and down. "Four hours until lift off. What are you meant to wear to a rooftop party, anyway?"

"Wear what makes you comfortable," Dina told her. "You don't need to wear something expensive to impress Callie. Just wear what you'd usually wear to a party – something elegant."

"Elegant," Sophie said dubiously, looking down at her scruffy Converse and ripped jeans.

Dina patted her knee. "Boys have got it so easy. All they need to do is put on a tuxedo and bow tie and – BAM! – job done. You four? Not so easy. We're going to need to create some looks."

Elisha sighed. "I think I ought to sit this one out."

The other girls looked at her with worried faces. "What's the matter?" Sophie asked. "Are you not

feeling very well?"

Elisha shook her head.

"Just not used to going to parties, huh?" Gabby asked.

Elisha laughed. "Guess you've never been to a Muslim wedding? Trust me – we know how to party in India. I don't want to be a party pooper. It's just . . . oh, how do I put this . . . my mathematician's intuition! Yes, that's it! Something doesn't add up."

"I think I know what you mean," Marie said, realising that she did. Something had felt not quite right today. She couldn't put her finger on it. When had she first felt it? Something Rosa had said . . .

"Too bad, Elisha. I thought you'd want to chat to that nice footballer from Manchester," Dina said. "What's his name? Marky Dashcam, something like that."

"*He's* going?" Elisha shot up from the sofa.

Dina waved her phone. "That's what your friend

Hayley Mackenzie says."

Elisha looked around the room. "What are you all waiting for? Let's get ready! We've got a party to go to!"

Chapter Six

Four hours later, Marie was wishing they had opted out after all. The rooftop party was *terrible*. Everyone there seemed shallow and fake, snapping selfies, updating their social media and showing off their wealth. She thought she caught sight of a few Hollywood stars and a musician or two, but they were all surrounded by huddles of people. All the girls could do was stick together in a tight group of their own and try to style it out.

"At least the food's good," Sophie said. "Vegan vol-au-vent, anyone?"

"No thanks," Marie sighed.

"Suit yourself. I'm going to get some punch," Sophie said through a mouthful of pastry.

Marie looked around for Callie, but there was still no sign of her. From the size of the crowd over by the rooftop dance floor, she was probably somewhere among them.

A piercing voice called, "Hey, girls! Having fun?" It was Hayley McKenzie again, holding up her phone as if she couldn't bear to leave a single moment uncaptured on video.

Marie gave her best charming smile. "Oh, you know how it is. Once you've been to one millionaire's party, you've been to all of them."

Hayley chuckled. "Tired of the celeb lifestyle already, huh? Just don't forget about coming on my channel tomorrow!"

From across the rooftop came an outraged squawk and a cry of, "Oh, jeez, I'm sorry!"

Marie saw, to her horror, that Sophie had accidentally spilled punch all over herself and the famous woman standing next to her. The woman was fairly short, with a high ponytail. She held up a sleeve dripping with red.

Marie grabbed Gabby's arm. "Oh my God, is that . . ."

Gabby was ashen. "Poor Sophie. She'll be scarred for life. She'll never be able to listen to her music again."

Marie caught sight of Callie at last. She was standing in a milling crowd of onlookers. Marie recognised a TV actor, the singer from a boy band and a comedian her mum liked. She waved across to Callie, who glanced her way for a second and then went back to chatting. Marie felt her heart sink.

"This is awful," she told Gabby. "Why did Callie bother inviting us at all if she was just going to spend the evening schmoozing with the celebs?"

"I've had more fun playing spades in my cousin's

kitchen," Gabby said.

"She was so nice earlier!" Marie felt suddenly angry. "You know what? I wish we could just bundle Callie into a taxi and drive her somewhere these people would never find her."

Gabby said, "I guess it isn't up to her. She won't have much of a choice in where she goes and what she does. Specially not with Rosa the watchdog hanging round her all the time."

Marie made up her mind to talk to Callie. She knocked back her glass of grape fizz, pretending it was champagne, so she'd feel brave, and strode over. She nearly crashed into Hayley MacKenzie, who was still recording footage on her phone.

Callie looked straight at Marie as she approached, and Marie immediately knew something was wrong. The look on Callie's face was pure misery. Her eyes were

shadowy and her mouth was tightly shut as if to keep the tears at bay.

"Callie, what is it? What's the matter?"

Rosa stepped into Marie's path, blocking Callie out altogether. "Run along, little girl," she said. "Do not interfere."

At that exact moment, Sophie came hurrying up to Marie, her dress soaked in punch. She was dabbing at it with a single wad of soaked tissue.

"Have you got any tissues, Marie?" Sophie begged.

"Come on," said Marie. She took Sophie's hand and dragged her over towards the toilets. They pushed through the crowds to the sinks. Marie unrolled a pile of toilet paper and went to work cleaning Sophie up.

"Thanks, but I still look like a murder victim." Sophie said as Marie helped her dry off under the hand dryer.

Marie sighed. "No problem. Look, this party's a bit of

a bust. Shall we just go?"

"Thought you'd never ask."

Marie opened the toilet door. There, frozen to the spot on the other side, gripping her phone like a dagger, was Callie Sunny. If she'd looked upset before, she looked downright dreadful now. Her face was pale and trembling.

Marie took a step forward. "Oh my God, Callie, what is it? Talk to me!"

Callie opened her mouth and shut it again. Her phone pinged with an incoming text. She checked the message and suddenly burst into tears.

"What's wrong? You can tell me!" Marie assured her.

Suddenly Rosa was there, appearing from behind, stern and silent. She put her arm on Callie's shoulder.

Callie gave Marie one last tearful look. Her hands quickly flashed up in a cryptic signal. Eight fingers. Then

five fingers. Then . . .

Rosa grabbed Callie's hand before she could make the final gesture. And away the pair of them went, disappearing into the crowd of celebrities.

"What was all that about?" Sophie wondered.

"I think Callie's in danger," Marie said. "Soph, find Gabby and Elisha, quick. Get to the ground floor and watch all the exits. Whatever's going on, we're going to stop it."

"Got it, Marie. What are you going to do?"

"I'm going to talk to Sterling Vance!"

Chapter Seven

Marie made her way through the party, hurriedly looking for Vance. He could always be found boasting to a crowd of people at his parties and this one wasn't any different. She found him at the far corner of the roof terrace gesturing with his drink to a group of bored-looking guests.

". . . and that's how I invented the GEMS. Years of work went into them . . ."

"Mr Vance," Marie interrupted. Vance shot her an annoyed look.

"I'm in the middle of a story, Marie. What do you want?" he retorted.

Marie took him to one side and whispered so that the guests wouldn't hear. "I'm sorry, Mr Vance, but you need to hear this. It's Callie Sunny. I think she's in danger. Someone's after her."

Vance didn't look convinced. "What makes you think that?"

Steadily, Marie explained what she'd seen. How Callie had been upset, then frightened, then reduced to tears by a text message. The weird hand signals. The way she seemed unable to speak. And Rosa, who seemed to have far too much control over her for a mere bodyguard.

Vance listened without interrupting. When Marie was done, he sighed. "Look, Marie, you're a good kid. But you're still a kid, understand? The adult world is all big and scary to you, and you're reading way too much into this. Callie's just having boy trouble or something."

"BOY trouble? Are you serious?"

"I'm paying for the very best security," Vance smoothly continued. "Rosa is reliable. She's an ex cage fighter, did you know that? Nobody's getting past her."

"I'm just saying, if you could send someone, check on Callie—"

"Maybe it's time you went home and got some sleep," Vance interrupted, with finality in his voice. "It'll be a big day tomorrow. Vance Expo officially opens at nine and you're supposed to be showing off the GEMS. Don't let me down."

He strode back into the centre of the party and launched into another of his stories.

Marie was so angry she stormed out of the party and made her way to the lobby in the lift. There were a few people milling around when she got there and she was still huffing over Vance not taking her seriously. There were Gabby, Elisha and Sophie, keeping an eye on the

doors like Marie had asked. She ran over to them.

"Have Callie or Rosa been through here?"

"We haven't seen them," Gabby said. "But you know there's two back ways out of here, right?"

"Three if you count the underground car park," said Elisha. Gabby groaned and slapped her forehead.

"So they could have left without us seeing. Or someone could have come in and left with Callie," said Sophie. "She could be anywhere by now."

"Elisha, Gabby, we need to tell you about something Callie did," said Marie. "Just before Rosa dragged her off, she held up her fingers like *this*."

"Eight, five, something? I don't get it," said Gabby and stroked her chin.

"I do," Elisha said instantly. "This way!"

Elisha ran across the lobby as if she was sprinting across a football pitch and dived into the lift before the

doors could close. She held them open for the other girls and thumbed the lift button marked 8 for the eighth floor.

"Well?" Marie's heart was pounding as they passed the third floor. "What does it mean?"

"All the rooms in this hotel have three digit numbers," Elisha said. "Eight five something. It's a room number. Callie was trying to tell you which room in the hotel she was staying in!"

They passed the fifth floor.

Marie's mouth fell open. "Of course! Why didn't I see it?" She pulled out her phone and sent Vance a text: MEET US 8TH FLOOR. CALLIE'S ROOM. URGENT!

They passed the seventh floor. The girls faced the doors. Any second now they would open.

"What do we do if Rosa tries to taser us?" asked Sophie.

"We can get around her if we have to," Gabby said,

adopting her best fighting pose. "I'm nimble like a ninja."

"My dad made me take Aikido classes when I was getting picked on at school," said Elisha sheepishly.

Marie, whose only fighting experience was from her unsuccessful attempts to wrangle Izzy into a bath, said nothing. The doors slid open. A seemingly normal hotel corridor lay before them.

Bracing themselves for a confrontation with Rosa, they headed towards the rooms numbered 850 to 859. Marie saw something up ahead and hissed at them to stop.

The door numbered 858 was open. Someone was lying on the floor.

Her whole body shaking, Marie crept forwards. The door led into a huge suite. A body – yes, it was definitely a human body – was lying face-down on the floor. Marie knew who it was before she even noticed the stinger

85

clutched in her hand.

"It's Rosa!"

A red light was blinking on the stinger's side. Thoughts raced through Marie's mind. Had Rosa tried to fend off an attacker?

Sophie bent down to check that Rosa was alright. The others stepped over her and into the room.

There was no sign of Callie anywhere. Random possessions were strewn across the floor inside the room. The waste bin was stuffed with roses. On the bed lay a dress, ripped and torn in several places, as if someone had hacked at it with savage fury. Something was scrawled on the dresser mirror in blood-red lipstick.

The girls frantically searched for Callie. Marie threw the bathroom door open. Nothing.

Meanwhile, Gabby pulled the closets open one by one. There was nothing inside but loose clothing and

magazines. Then one of the closet doors rattled in Gabby's grip. "Locked," she said.

Marie took one look at the closet. Yes, it was big enough to hide someone inside. Without thinking, she kicked it. It didn't give. *This isn't a movie*, Marie thought. *It'll take more than just one kick.*

She slammed kick after kick into the closet door until the wood split and caved in. Marie expected to see Callie inside, taken prisoner – but she wasn't. There was nothing in there but a laptop tucked on top of a shelf.

"She's coming round," Sophie said.

Rosa groaned and moved her leg. She tried to sit up, fell back down again, gasped, and tried again. Sophie offered her a hand, but Rosa irritably slapped it away. She got to her feet just as Sterling Vance appeared at the doorway.

He looked in through the door, saw the mess and

physically flinched. "Holy . . . what *happened* here?"

"You need to call the police," Marie urged him.

Looking numb, Vance moved through the room towards the dresser. For the first time, Marie read the lipstick message. It read: THIS WILL COST STERLING VANCE MILLIONS.

"It's a ransom demand," he choked. "She's been kidnapped. Callie's been taken!"

"Get off me!" Rosa yelled, pushing Sophie away. "I don't need your help!"

Vance pointed a shaking finger. "You. You were meant to be her bodyguard. What the hell happened to you?"

"I don't know!" Rosa snapped and rubbed her neck.

"Not good enough," said Vance. "Talk."

Rosa closed her eyes and concentrated. "I was in my room next door, I came through to check on Callie,

and sat down by the dresser. Callie was on the bed. She wanted to try on the dress for the big concert."

Marie glanced over at the remains of the dress on the bed.

"Someone knocked on the door. I got up, checked the spyhole, didn't see anyone. Figured it was the cleaner. I opened the door a crack, looked down the hall . . . and something like a hornet stung me on the neck. Everything went black. Next thing I know, this kid is pawing at me." She glared at Sophie.

"Sounds like they used a ranged stun gun on you," Vance said. "Sloppy of you, Rosa. The kidnappers must have stepped over you and taken Callie."

"Callie would have fought them, though!" Marie said.

"They probably stunned her too," Rosa said. "Then bundled her out of here. Which means we're looking for at least two people."

This was all getting way too serious, Marie thought. She pulled out her phone. "Mr Vance, if you don't call the police right now, I'll do it myself."

"No," said Vance.

"Fine."

Marie began to type 999, but Vance grabbed her wrist. "You can't get the police involved, because you four would be the number one suspects!"

"What?" the four girls yelled together.

Vance brandished his own phone. "This was uploaded just moments ago. Kind of convenient, don't you think?"

The phone screen showed Hayley MacKenzie's YouTube channel, with a new video called *Chilling with Callie and Friends* playing. Marie was shocked to see it was the footage Hayley had shot earlier that evening. And there was Marie herself, saying something angrily. Vance turned up the volume so they could all hear:

"I wish we could just bundle Callie into a taxi and drive her somewhere these people would never find her!"

"But ... but I didn't mean kidnap her!" she stammered.

Vance played it again. " *... bundle Callie into a taxi ... never find her ..."*

"*Chica*, it doesn't matter what you meant," said Gabby. "Cops can twist your words any way they want. Think about it. Our fingerprints are all over the room now. You kicked the closet door through! No way they won't bring us in."

"But we know we didn't do it!" Marie insisted.

"Yes," Vance explained, "but the police *don't* know that – and while they're wasting time investigating the four of you, the real culprit will be getting away!"

"So what do we do?" Sophie demanded.

Vance looked at the ransom demand again. "We're

going to have to keep this quiet. There's nothing else for it. I'll put together a cover story and field any questions from the press."

Marie asked, "And what about us?"

"I'm going to need the four of you to work together like never before. You'll need every bit of science skill you've got. Any equipment you need, I'll pay for."

"Mr Vance, you can't seriously be asking us to . . ." Marie's voice trailed off.

Vance looked her right in the eye. "That's right. I need you girls to find Callie Sunny."

Chapter Eight

Rosa let out a harsh laugh. "You think *they* will find her? Little girls playing detective? I do not think so."

"Go on and call the police, then," Marie said defiantly.

The bodyguard made a disgusted face. "British police? Incompetent. I would not think of involving them. They would only screw it up." She turned to leave. "I will find Callie Sunny myself, and I will do it before any of you."

As Rosa was heading out of the door, Marie called after her: "Wait! Work with us. You spent more time with Callie than anyone. You could be a real help."

Rosa snarled down at her. "This is your one and only warning. Stay out of my way! I am a professional,

understand? I don't need a bunch of amateurs slowing me down." She turned to Vance. "Sir. You know I am reliable. If I leave now, I might be able to catch up with the abductors."

"Go." Vance made a flicking gesture with his fingers.

As Rosa ran from the room, Marie kept her eyes on Vance, judging his reaction. "Mr Vance, I don't trust her."

"Why?"

"I'm sure she's keeping something back from us."

Gabby nodded. "She's covering something up. I can guess why. It's her fault Callie was taken. I bet she wasn't even watching properly."

Vance pondered that, then shook his head. "I'm going to my room. I need to think. You four, get investigating. And hurry up, won't you? If Rosa returns she'll kick you all out – and she could come back at any minute."

He handed Marie a platinum credit card. "In case you

need equipment. Or anything else."

The door closed, and the four girls were left alone in the crime scene.

Marie thought of Callie, alone and afraid somewhere. *She's counting on us,* she thought. *We're not the people she would have picked to find her, but we're the ones she's got. We have to do this and do it right.*

She clapped her hands, jolting the others to attention. "OK, gang. We've only got a few minutes. Everyone take their own part of the suite. If you find anything that might be a clue, take a picture with your phone. If it's something we can bring with us, then grab it."

The girls got to work. Minute by minute, centimetre by centimetre, they searched the rooms and tried to make sense of the scene. There was no sign that any kind of a fight had taken place. Apart from the torn-up dress on the bed and the door Marie had kicked

in herself, nothing was broken. Marie was glad there was nothing to suggest Callie had been hurt. Rosa was probably right, she would have been stunned as well.

By the time they were done, they had found a long straggly wig, Callie's shredded dress, a bunch of red-gold roses that were in the rubbish bin, a ripped celebrity gossip magazine and the laptop that Marie had found in the closet. Gabby took photos of the ransom note written in lipstick on the mirror.

"Do you think this is enough?" Sophie asked.

"It'll have to be," Marie said. "It's all we've got."

Back at Marie's house, the four girls rushed past Dina and her questions about how their night had been and ran straight into the Inventing Shed. Marie put up a

pinboard on the wall. They would use the shed as their crime lab.

"What's that for?" Elisha asked.

"So we can put pictures up with circles and arrows on, to figure out what happened," said Marie. "It's what they do in detective shows."

Marie cleared off her workbench and they laid out all the gathered evidence. The obvious object to start with was the laptop. Gabby flipped it open and the screen immediately asked for a password. She muttered something rude under her breath and typed a few characters. The screen flashed up: PASSWORD INCORRECT.

"Can you hack it?" Marie asked.

"Oh, sure, but it'll take time. And time we don't have," Gabby said. "Ugh, these so-called clues! A wig? And who brought the magazine? Looks like trash."

"Me," said Elisha. "I think Callie tore it up."

Marie fingered the torn magazine pages. "Maybe if we put them back together . . . Sophie, can you pass me that sticky tape?"

Marie set to work sticking the ripped magazine back together. As the pages took shape she started to see the headline of the story coming together. She began to work faster, feeling as if Callie was reaching out and talking to her through the print.

"Done," she said. "And you're all going to want to read this."

The headline read: PHOEBE POISON LAYS INTO CALLIE SUNNY – WE SPILL THE TEA!

"Phoebe Poison?" Gabby said. "The singer? I've heard of her. She's really nasty. I'm talking reduce grown men to tears kind of *nasty*. And they're saying *she* has beef with Callie? Poor Callie!"

"Serious beef, by the sound of it," Marie said. She read the story out loud to the others. Phoebe Poison was accusing Callie of being a fake and a sellout, who had turned her back on her real fans. "'Not to mention everything else she's done – she knows, and I know she knows, but I ain't saying.'" At the end was a warning not to come to London, since it was Phoebe's territory. "'And if you do, I won't be responsible for the consequences!'"

"And Callie ignored the warning," Marie finished. "This magazine's from yesterday. Do you think Phoebe Poison could have had Callie kidnapped?"

"Of course she could!" Sophie yelled. "All that stuff about 'respect' and 'consequences'. What other explanation is there?"

Elisha folded her hands in her lap and looked very thoughtful. "We know Phoebe hates Callie. And she has money and a big crew of people surrounding her. She's

definitely a suspect."

"And Phoebe would totes have torn up Callie's dress, too!" Gabby said, with a look to Elisha as if that settled it.

Marie took the picture of Phoebe Poison from the magazine and pinned it to the top of her board. "OK. Suspect number one. What now?"

"We've still got too many questions," said Gabby. "What I want to know is, how did the kidnappers sneak up on Rosa, and how did they get Callie out of the building?"

Marie groaned. "I don't even know where to start!"

Sophie said, "Maybe look at it backwards? If you had to do all those things and get away with it, how would you do them?"

Marie racked her brains. *Think*, she said to herself. *How can you come up to a hotel room door without being noticed? How can you leave again with more*

than you brought?

"Cleaners," she said. "That could be it! If the hotel cleaners came up to the door, Rosa wouldn't suspect them. And they could have wheeled Callie away in a laundry trolley!"

"Down the service elevator, where nobody else would go," Elisha said.

Marie eagerly wrote *Disguised as cleaners?* on the board. *Detection was a lot like inventing,* she thought. *It was all about trial and error, dead ends and sudden breakthroughs.*

She noticed Sophie was staring moodily at the floor. "Soph, are you OK? What's up?"

"Oh, it's stupid," Sophie said.

Gabby put an arm round her shoulder. "Nothing's stupid right now. What's the matter?"

"I can't believe she threw those lovely roses in the

bin!" Sophie burst out. "Poor flowers. They didn't do anything wrong. Why throw them away?"

Marie held up a hand. "Hang on. Why *would* Callie treat those beautiful roses that way?"

Gabby shrugged. "She obviously didn't want them."

"Right, but why?"

"I don't know? Maybe she was allergic."

"Or maybe it has something to do with who sent them," Elisha suggested.

Marie decided to take a closer look. Taking care to avoid the thorns on the stems, she carefully prised the mangled bunch of roses apart. She noticed for the first time that the colour was unusual. Instead of being deep red, the flower heads were reddish-gold and glistened where they caught the light.

"Soph, do you know what sort of roses these are?" she asked. "I've never seen any roses this colour."

"Now you mention it, no. At first, I thought they might even be fake, but they're not, are they?" said Sophie.

A flash of ivory caught Marie's eye. Tucked between the stems was a gift card. Marie tugged it free and unfolded it. "It's a handwritten note!"

"That means those roses were delivered in person," Elisha said immediately.

"Right! Because when you get flowers delivered from a company, they print the message. And they have company letterheads and stuff," chimed in Gabby.

Marie held the note up to the light. It was covered in neat and formal handwriting.

Sophie stood up excitedly. "Well, don't keep us in suspense! What does it say?"

"Oh God. I think Callie had a stalker," said Marie.

"What?" the other three chorused.

Marie held the note at arm's length as if it were

something rotten. "Listen to this. 'I must add you to my garden. Only I can take proper care of you. From your most devoted admirer, your one and only, Q.C.'"

Chapter Nine

The next morning, Marie stood at the GEMS booth surrounded by the crazy bustle of Vance Expo. All sorts of people were coming up to her, marvelling at the tiny robots and making astonished noises that four young girls could have invented them. She smiled and nodded politely back at them but her mind was still on the night before.

It seemed almost like a dream. Images flashed through Marie's mind: a tearful face, a shredded dress, Rosa's unconscious body. Callie Sunny really had been kidnapped. They really had sat in the Inventing Shed puzzling over clues until almost midnight. But no matter

how hard it might be, they still had to get through today.

At midday, they headed up to the Executive Lounge. Sterling Vance was waiting at a private table for them, with food already prepared. He gestured for them to keep their voices down. "Well, how's the investigation going?" he asked immediately.

"We've already got two suspects," Marie said. "Someone called Q.C. – we don't know who that is – and a rival musician. Phoebe Poison."

Vance dropped the stick of celery he was dipping in hummus, and quickly swabbed at his mouth with a napkin. "I've heard of Phoebe. I don't want you going after her. She's dangerous."

"But she's our number one suspect!" Sophie protested.

"I said to drop it," Vance ordered them, glowering. "You don't know who you're messing with. Besides, I'm sure Miss Poison doesn't have anything to do with

Callie going missing so leave it alone!"

Just as Marie was about to voice her dismay, Vance glanced past her and gave a tight-lipped smile. "Ah! Camilla. Please join us."

A woman in a sharp business suit came gliding up to their table and sat down. "Sterling, dear. And these must be your apprentices. How nice."

The moment Marie saw her, she felt her skin crawl. It was the same unease she'd felt yesterday when she had accidentally found herself talking to an android. From head to toe, everything about Camilla screamed 'fake'. Her nails, her clothes, her sweetly smarmy manner. Marie wouldn't have been surprised if her face had fallen off and revealed a panel of wires and circuits with wobbly eyeballs.

"Camilla is Callie Sunny's brand director," said Vance. "What's a brand director?" said Elisha suspiciously.

Camilla gave a shrill laugh. "Oh, sweetie. To be so young and innocent!"

"A brand director helps to decide what a product's image and message are going to be," explained Vance.

Marie pushed her food away unfinished. "And Callie is your *product*, is she?"

Camilla laid her cold fingers on Marie's wrist, making her flinch. She said, "Callie is my daughter."

Vance looked right at Marie, and his expression said, *say nothing.*

It was all Marie could do to keep down the little food she'd eaten. She wasn't sure what was worse – knowing that this dreadful woman was her friend's mother, or having to keep quiet about Callie having gone missing. She could just about understand Vance keeping that information from the police, but from Callie's own mum?

"Camilla's only in town for a couple of hours," said

Vance, appearing unfazed.

"But I'll be back on the night of the big concert, of course," Camilla added. "I'm sure it'll be a stupendous success. All that hard work is finally going to pay off."

Marie thought to herself: *if we can't find Callie in time, there isn't going to BE a concert! What will Vance do then?*

As the uncomfortable lunch went on, Camilla chatted away, regardless of whether anyone was listening. Most of what she had to say was praise for herself, and the rest was criticism of everyone else. By the time Sterling Vance had munched his way through his salad, Camilla had lectured Elisha for being too quiet, Sophie for being too loud and "dressing like one of those awful granola moms", Gabby for wearing too much make-up and even Vance for not dyeing out the grey in his hair. "I know you think it makes you look distinguished, but darling,

you're starting to look like a creepy old man," she said.

At least she hasn't picked on me yet, Marie thought.

But just then, Camilla said, "Now, Marie, have you ever thought of going to a finishing school? I'm sure Sterling would pay for it."

Stay calm, Marie told herself. "A finishing school? You mean . . . to learn which fork to use with the fish, and how to speak to royals?"

"Of course. You're a little rough diamond, I know, but you're far too outspoken. You could do with a lesson in manners."

Vance cleared his throat. "Camilla, I don't think—"

"Oh, no offence meant, I assure you," Camilla said, giving Marie a smile that stretched her Botoxed skin like plastic wrap. "It's not Marie's fault. She didn't choose her family."

Marie churned inwardly with a combination of

injured pride, humiliation and anger. How dare this woman think she was better than Marie just because of her wealth? *Lucky for you I was brought up right, and I do know how to mind my manners!* she thought.

"No, I didn't choose my family," Marie said. "I was blessed with them. And every day I'm grateful."

Camilla rapidly changed the subject. "So, Vance. How has Callie has been behaving? I trust she hasn't been giving you any bother?"

"Not really," Vance said. "Though I do need to bring you up to speed on something. I, uh—"

"That bodyguard you hired seems like a bad influence to me," Camilla interrupted. "You do know she has a criminal background, don't you?"

Marie made a mental note of that and imagined herself writing it on her investigation pinboard. Rosa had a criminal past? What had she done?

Vance sighed. "Look, Camilla, there's no easy way to say this, so I'm just going to cut to the chase. Callie has gone missing."

Camilla screwed her napkin into a ball and flung it on to the table. "I knew it. I knew something must have happened!"

"But I promise you, I have my very best people looking for her. It'll all work out fine. We just need to stay calm."

Camilla stood up. "Damn you, Sterling Vance," she hissed. "I swear to God, if anything happens to Callie, I will sue you for every penny you've got. You have no idea what I've done . . . what sacrifices I've made! I am not going to let you throw all of that away!"

She stormed away from the table.

Vance leaned back in his chair and loosened his tie. "That went about as badly as it could have," he said. "Girls, don't bother going back to the GEMS booth today.

I'll get some staffers to look after it. I need you hunting for Callie."

Back in the Inventing Shed, the girls felt under more pressure than ever. Each of them chose a lead to follow. Marie looked for people with the initials Q.C. who might have a grudge against Callie. Gabby patiently tried to bypass the password protection on Callie's laptop. Sophie studied the roses to work out what strain they were, and Elisha drew careful diagrams of the hotel room to try to reconstruct the events. Marie wished they could have investigated Phoebe Poison, but Vance had warned them off her and she didn't want to cross him right now.

"That Camilla woman wasn't making empty threats,"

Sophie said. "If we don't get Callie back, VanceCorp is as good as hers. And I don't want to work for her!"

"Did you hear how she talked about Callie?" Marie mused. "Like an investment! How can she treat her daughter like some kind of object, instead of a person?"

From the corner of the room came a triumphant shout. "Aw, yeah! We're in!"

Gabby had cracked the password! The girls crowded round to see what was on it.

"No documents, no pictures, not even any music . . . aha, here's a phone finder app! That could lead us right to her. Hmm . . . nothing. I guess her phone's not switched on. Oh, hey, she's still logged in to her social media accounts." Gabby pulled up Callie's private messages. "Let's see what folks have been sending her."

"Wait," said Elisha. "Are you sure we should be doing this? Aren't we invading her privacy?"

Marie thought back to how Callie had looked at her with tears streaming down her face and said, "We have to. It's the only way we can help her."

Gabby clicked. Instantly, they saw a string of comments on Callie's profile. They had come in at different times, but they all said much the same thing:

You're a FAKE!

Sell out. How can u face ur fans after this?

LOSER

Imagine liking Callie Sunny, lol

Go cry to mamma and never come back!

On and on they went, for page after page.

"Who's sending them?" Marie asked.

Gabby checked. "Burner accounts. You know – obvious fake names, no profile picture. But going by the style and the timing . . . I think it's probably almost all from the same person."

"Maybe that's what Callie saw that made her burst into tears. One too many of these," Marie said. If so, Marie couldn't blame her. What must it be like to have people hurling hate at you like this?

Elisha wrote a new question on the pinboard: *Who sent the nasty comments?*

The Inventing Shed was growing stuffy with all four of them working so hard. Marie needed some air. She headed out into her back garden and looked up into the peaceful night sky. The stars were starting to come out overhead.

"How I wonder what you are," she whispered to herself, looking at one faint, faraway star.

She'd never really thought about it before, but it was

strange that famous people were called 'stars'. Was it because they were out of ordinary people's reach? Or because they were looked to for guidance? *Maybe it's because they look beautiful from far off, but up close they're raging furnaces of nuclear chaos, either blowing up or collapsing on themselves,* she thought to herself.

"Hold tight, Callie. We're going to find you," she promised.

The Inventing Shed door flew open. "Marie!" Gabby called. "Sophie's done it. We've found him. Our first real lead!"

"What?" Marie followed her inside.

Sophie pointed at her laptop screen. "I've identified the exact species of rose! Get this. It's a unique strain called Morning Sunrise, and it's grown right here in London."

Marie gasped. "Find out who sells them!"

"Already have," said Sophie. "There's only one florist in the whole city where you can buy Morning Sunrise. This guy's the owner."

"Look at his name!" said Elisha.

Marie read the name off the screen. "Oh my God. 'Quentin Crump.' That's him. He's Q.C.!"

Chapter Ten

The florist's shop front looked run down and shabby, as if it received few visitors. Security gratings closed off the front windows. The rest of the building looked like a large house, its peaked roofs, iron spires and narrow windows reminding Marie of the sort of place witches lived in in children's stories. She and the girls watched it from the other side of the street.

"The upstairs light's on, so someone's home," Marie said.

"Should we go and knock?" asked Sophie.

"No way," said Elisha. "Right now he doesn't know we're coming. That's our only advantage."

"Let's stake him out," suggested Gabby. "Watch the house, see what he does."

Marie nodded agreement. This might be a seriously dangerous situation, but they had to investigate, for Callie's sake. "All right. Round the back, then."

They crossed the road and found the narrow alleyway that led round to the backs of the houses. Tall clapboard fences, closed the gardens off, and wheelie bins stood haphazardly along the way. There was no mistaking Crump's back yard. A gigantic conservatory almost filled it up completely.

Marie said, "I'm not an expert, but . . . isn't the whole point of a conservatory to let light in, not keep it out?"

All the glass panes were solid black.

Gabby whistled. "Gee, Mr Crump, that's not suspicious at *all*."

"Why would you black out the windows?" said Marie.

"To hide what you've got inside," said Sophie gravely. "Or who."

Marie grabbed the fence, tried to climb up, and scrabbled helplessly with her boots on the planks. "One of you give me a leg-up," she gasped. "We've got to get inside that conservatory!"

Gabby shoved her foot up from beneath and Marie suddenly found herself tumbling over the wall and down the other side. She landed hard in a flower bed. A rose bush dragged a painful scratch down her leg, and before her eyes it began to bead with blood. She crammed her knuckles into her mouth to keep from yelling.

"Marie, are you OK?" whispered Gabby from behind the wall.

"Fine!" Marie lied. She checked the wooden door. Not padlocked, thank goodness, but that rusty bolt

could make a loud screech if she wasn't careful, and then Crump would catch them. Summoning all the concentration she could muster, she carefully worked the bolt up and down and back and forth until she had worried it free. The door swung open and the other girls crept into the garden.

"We're trespassing," whispered Sophie.

"And if we find Callie tied up in there, you think anyone's going to care about that?" snapped Gabby.

"Guys," said Elisha meaningfully, and beckoned them over. She was crouching down beside a grimy window.

Careful to stay out of sight, Marie edged up to the window. Elisha caught her eye and gave her a nod. She peered through.

A sweaty, pale, rather flabby-looking man was standing at the cooker hob, stirring a huge pan full of something glistening and dark. He wore a string vest,

his head was bald except for the bits above his ears, and his round glasses looked like the lenses out of Marie's telescope. She was looking at him from the side; he hadn't seen her yet, but if he looked to his right, he would.

"Dinnertime, my precious," he said to himself in a sing-song voice, and banged the spoon on the side of the pan. He picked the pan up and turned in Marie's direction. She jerked out of sight, her heart hammering, her breath tight in her chest.

"It's definitely him," she whispered to the others. "He's got her."

She heard the sound of shuffling feet slip-slapping on a lino floor as Crump moved through to the conservatory. Moments later, the thumping sound of music came from inside. Marie felt cold torrents gush through her veins. She knew that music.

"That's *My Friends Call Me Medusa*," she whispered. "He's playing one of Callie's songs on a sound system!"

"He must be taking that stew through to feed to her. I bet it's got stuff in it to make her sleepy," said Elisha.

Gabby cracked her knuckles. "There goes the very last little itty bit of doubt I had. C'mon, girls. Let's put this creep on the front page."

"So how do we get in?" said Sophie.

The four of them quickly checked out the back of the house. Marie stepped on a fragment of flowerpot that broke with a jarring crack, but there was no response from inside. *At least the sound of Callie's music is covering up any noise we might make,* Marie thought. It was an unexpected bonus.

The conservatory door was locked, of course. The back door of the house itself was locked too. A window on the upper floor was wide open, but the walls were

sheer and there was no way up to it. Just as it looked like they would have to give up, Gabby found a little oblong window slightly ajar.

"We're going in through the toilet window?" said Marie in horror.

"If we fit," Gabby said.

Elisha stepped forward. "I'll go. I'm the only one of us small enough."

Sophie and Marie helped Elisha scramble up and squeeze through the tiny gap. For a moment she hung there, kicking her legs, grunting and gasping with the effort. From inside came the sound of a closing door. Marie got ready to pull Elisha back out, thinking that Crump was on the move, but she slid through with a little yelp and a crash and clatter of falling bottles.

We're finished, thought Marie. She kept very still. Her leg stung where the thorn had scratched it. Heartbeat

followed heartbeat. And then, slowly, the back door began to open. Marie braced herself to confront Crump.

But it was Elisha who popped her head out. "I unlocked it. Get in, quick!"

"You're awesome!" Marie told her as they crept inside.

Marie slowly made her way into the gloomy kitchen, her heart pounding like a drum.

A single bare lightbulb lit the room. The sink was piled with dirty plates. Old window boxes were stacked on every surface. The air stank of potting compost and something else – a thick, sweetly sour, tarry smell that reminded Marie of the school biology lab. It made her eyes water.

Every surface, every crooked shelf and filthy worktop, was covered with plants. They looked twisted, as if some evil force had corrupted them. Marie saw thorns as long as her thumb, bloated pods, drooping

dark green tendrils.

One door led back into the guts of the house, another looked like it must lead to the conservatory. The muffled sound of Callie's music came from behind the conservatory door. Marie quickly tried to think up a plan. "Everyone get your phones ready. We need to catch him on video so he can't lie his way out of this."

She took a deep breath – and next moment, it burst out of her in a scream. The door was opening. Pale, wet eyes stared into hers.

Crump stood frozen to the spot, a wooden spoon in his hands. As he looked at the girls grouped together in his kitchen his mouth plopped open like a blobfish.

Marie felt sudden anger surge through her. It made it easy to do what she had to do. She strode right up to Crump. "What have you done with Callie Sunny?" she demanded, looking him dead in the eye.

Crump's face shuddered like a pudding and for a second he seemed about to cry. Then he let out a bloodcurdling scream and ran. He pushed past Marie and made for the kitchen door, slipping and skidding on the lino. Then he was gone.

"Find Callie!" Marie yelled over her shoulder and took off after Crump.

She ran through into the garden. The door to the back alley was still open. Crump dived through it and flung it shut behind him. The latch closed with a smart *clack*. Cursing, Marie grabbed the handle, fumbled the latch open again and dived after him. She'd lost crucial seconds.

She ran out into the alley and glanced left and right. No sign of Crump. He wouldn't have had time to run further down the alley behind the other houses, so he must have gone the other way into the street.

Marie started off that way, but then a crash made her turn around. Crump had been hiding behind one of the wheelie bins, and now he had pulled it down to block her path. Marie yelled in frustration and ran after him again.

Crump sprinted down the alleyway, pulling bins over to either side. Someone in one of the houses yelled 'Oi!'. Crump glanced over his shoulder, saw Marie was dogging his heels, and put on a burst of speed. Marie jumped right over the wheelie bin in her path, landed, stumbled – *ouch!* – and kept on after him.

He was nearly at the end of the alley now. Marie was sure she'd never catch him if he got out of her sight. Crump seemed to think the same thing, because he raised his arms like an Olympic runner and began to dash the last hundred yards as if his life depended on it.

But Marie wasn't letting him get away. She leapt

over another wheelie bin, nearly skidded in the rubbish that had spilled out of it and ran as hard as she could. A memory of school sports day flashed across her mind, and her parents cheering her on from the sidelines.

Crump was only a few feet from the end of the alley. Suddenly he came to a staggering stop and let out a wail of terror as Elisha came running around the corner, lifting a shovel like it was a battle axe. Marie wanted to cheer. Elisha must have gone around the front!

Marie and Elisha closed in on Crump from opposite sides. Crump sank to his knees and buried his face in his hands. It was over.

Chapter Eleven

Marie, Elisha, Gabby and Sophie stood in Crump's conservatory, bathed in the weird light of the cultivation lamps. Rows of roses lay before them, twining up in unnatural shapes. Roses with heads the size of cabbages; roses with leaves like pearly silver tinged with pink; roses as soft and black as panther fur. Nearby lay a saucepan full of dark, smelly liquid.

On a side table, a Bluetooth speaker was still blasting Callie Sunny's music. Crump went and turned it off and looked at the girls with sorrowful eyes.

"What do you want with me?" he said.

"We want to know where Callie is," replied Marie.

"I don't know," said Crump. His voice was like something crawling over wet leaves. "I wish I did. She's in terrible danger."

Gabby laughed in disbelief. "What? We thought you'd kidnapped her!"

"Me?" Crump boggled. "Never! Kidnapped, you say? Is she all right? Is this why you broke into my house and chased me?"

"You were stalking her. You sent her roses just like those," said Marie quickly, pointing to the golden-red blooms.

Crump stroked the roses' heads lovingly. "My finest creation. Only the best for Callie Sunny. I'm her number one fan, but I wouldn't expect you to know that. You don't understand her like I do."

Elisha looked at Crump as if he was a maggot. "She threw your precious roses in the bin!"

Crump shrugged. "I can always grow more."

"Stop playing innocent," Marie said angrily. "When you sent her those roses you talked about 'adding her to your garden'! What was *that* about?"

Crump fell silent and Marie wondered if he was playing for time. But then he said, "There are some truly horrible people out there in the world. People who want Callie to fail. People who are jealous of her success. Like a precious bloom, she must be protected. Looked after. Cultivated."

"Kept prisoner, you mean," said Marie. "Gabby, Sophie, search the house again while Elisha and I keep an eye on this creep."

"She's not here!" Crump yelled, his voice rising to a shriek. "Besides, I've been at the Ottersbridge Flower Show for the past three days, and I can prove it! Please, you've got to hear me out."

He pulled out a ticket stub to the flower show from his pocket. The dates matched up.

Marie folded her arms and glared while Crump explained. "I'm not a stalker, whatever you might think," he said. "Just a deeply devoted fan. My conservatory is experimental. I create new strains of rose. That's not a crime, is it? Growing flowers?"

"What was that black liquid in the pan?" Elisha demanded.

"It's a special nutrient broth. My own invention. And before you ask . . . yes, I was playing Callie's music to the plants. It encourages them to grow."

Gabby sighed disgustedly. "He may be a weirdo, but I guess he's not a kidnapper."

Feeling dejected and a bit guilty, the girls got ready to leave. "Sorry, Mr Crump," Marie said. "But you can see how we thought you might be . . . well, you know."

"I could call the police on you right now," Crump said softly. "Give me one good reason why I shouldn't."

"Because you want to help Callie," Marie said.

Crump bowed his head. "I wish you'd tell me what has happened. I could help. But you're not going to, are you?"

"No," said Gabby.

"Back to square one," sighed Elisha.

Just as they were heading out through the front door, a sudden thought flashed across Marie's mind. She raced back inside the house. "Mr Crump?"

"Oh, what is it now?" Crump groaned.

"You said you wanted to protect Callie from 'them'. So ... who's 'them'?"

Crump turned his pale, watery gaze on her as if she was stupid. "The online trolls and haters, of course! Ever since Callie became famous, she's attracted a host of

ghastly, ignorant people. They've bombarded her with nasty messages on social media."

Marie returned to the girls and told them what he'd said. "That fits with what Gabby found on Callie's laptop!"

"Maybe one of the haters could have had it in for Callie," Elisha added.

"Hey, Crump!" Gabby yelled. "Who'd you say is the worst of all Callie's haters? The real king or queen of the trolls?"

"That's easy," Crump said, walking into the hallway with a little smile.

He waited, watching the girls' faces, and Marie thought: *now that we need him, he's gone smug again.* "Spit it out," she warned him.

"The very worst troll of all, in my opinion, would be 'Twinkle'. Horrible girl. All I know about her is that she

lives in Islington. She's said things to Callie that I cannot ever forgive."

Out in the street, Gabby confirmed what Crump had said. "A lot of the nasty comments on Callie's Insta were from Twinkle. I bet she has dozens of cover accounts, too."

"We've got a new lead," Sophie said brightly. "It's time to go troll hunting!"

"Not quite," said Elisha. "Have you all forgotten? We've got an appointment to keep. We're due on Hayley Mackenzie's show tonight!"

The girls sat together in Hayley's studio building, squeezed on to a squashy red sofa shaped like a pair of bright red lips. They were in 'the green room', though

it wasn't green at all. That was just what you called the room where people waited to go in front of the cameras. Or so Jeff, the producer, told them.

He poured them all glasses of iced water. Marie thought he was being a little too nice. "You're due on in ten," he said. "Any of you ever been on YouTube before?"

Nobody wanted to speak. Eventually Sophie said, "I gave a flower to Prince William when I was six, and it was on a local vloggers channel . . ." Her voice trailed off.

"Relax!" Jeff urged them. "You'll be fine! Have a chat among yourselves, get the buzz flowing." He went to talk to the crew members wheeling the cameras about.

"I can't believe we haven't planned this out," Gabby said.

Marie said, "Let's do it now. What message do we want to get across?"

All of them agreed they wanted to encourage other

kids like them to get into STEM subjects. Especially girls. But none of them were quite sure how to do that.

Sophie fidgeted. "I keep needing the loo. I'm so nervous."

"Me too," Marie said. "We just need to think about all the kids out there who need to see people like us on the screen. If we can help just one, it'll be worth it."

Jeff came to fetch them. "Guys, you're up! Break a leg!"

They followed him down a passage and walked into the glare of studio lights. Recorded cheering played over the speakers. Hayley was waiting for them on the set, which was a mock-up of a basement full of toys, games and gadgets.

"Welcome to the Anti-Boredom Agenda!" she told them.

Jeff, standing by the cameras, held up a sign reading SMILE! Marie beamed, Jeff gave her a thumbs up, and

gestured for her to go and sit down. *Here goes,* Marie thought. *Oh God.*

The four girls sat on one side of a glass table, with Hayley at the other. She introduced them all by name. It was just like the thousands of chat shows Marie had watched with her mum.

"These four lucky girls are apprentices at VanceCorp, and we'll be talking to them all about that," Hayley said, looking into the cameras. "Thanks for coming on, girls. You're an inspiration!"

"Thanks, Hayley. Great to be here," Marie said. *Wow, very original,* she scolded herself inwardly.

Hayley went on: "But before we talk science, let's put your skills to the test. We're going to play Mystery Objects! Can we have the trolley, please?"

The speakers played a cheesy crash of thunder and the lights flickered. An attendant dressed as a mad

scientist wheeled out a trolley. There were four covered plates on it, along with medical instruments. Marie's face fell. Jeff brandished the SMILE! sign again and she forced a grin.

"Your challenge is to identify the items!" Hayley said.

The attendant uncovered the first object, a white ball covered in diamond-shaped facets, and passed it to Elisha.

"It's a rhombic triacontahedron," she said instantly and gave it back.

"Gosh!" Hayley said, with a little laugh. "That didn't take long. Let's see if we can stump Marie."

The attendant handed Marie a piece of crumpled golden foil. She knew exactly what it was the moment she touched it. But she felt like she ought to play to the cameras a bit.

"A chocolate wrapper?" she said, with a goofy grin.

Hayley loved that. "Try again!"

Marie pretended to concentrate. Hayley said, "Here's a clue. Think of Katherine Johnson."

"It's Mylar foil," said Marie. "They used it on the moon landings as insulation."

The speakers played a blare of trumpets. Confetti fell from the ceiling and colourful balloons drifted down. Marie brushed confetti out of her braids, trying not to look too irritated.

"Well done!" said Hayley, clapping her hands. "Now, Gabriella?"

Gabby was given something like a long lightbulb. "It's an old electric valve," she said.

"Can you narrow it down any further?" said Hayley, leaning in.

Gabby said, "Hmm. Lots of machines used these, but I'm guessing you've given us objects based on our skills,

so . . . it's got to be a computer component. A really early one."

Riotous applause played over the speakers. "Spot on!" cheered Hayley. "It's actually from Colossus, the first true computer ever built. And it was made right here in Britain, in Bletchley Park! Three for three so far. Now, Sophie, can you tell us what this is?"

Sophie picked up a large, lumpy object the colour of dirty bone. "It's a tooth. A molar. Too big to be from a horse. I'm guessing . . . elephant?"

"Ooh, so close!" squealed Hayley. "Is that your final answer?"

Sophie peered at it. "Yup. It's definitely an elephant."

"Oh no," sighed Hayley, and the sound of a sad trombone parped in the background. "I'm sorry, Sophie but it's actually from a woolly mammoth, and it's thousands of years old!"

"No it isn't," said Sophie.

Hayley smiled sweetly. "I think you'll find—"

"The colour is all wrong," Sophie said. "This is from a modern elephant. Almost certainly illegally traded, too. Scammers sell fake fossils on Ebay all the time."

Jeff was looking anxiously at Hayley and making throat-cutting gestures.

"Oops! Looks like we need to have a word with our interns," Hayley said, and canned laughter drowned out the rest of what Sophie was trying to say.

Hayley took a deep breath. "Anyway, enough with all the nerd stuff. Let's move on to what the folks watching at home really want to know!"

Horrified, Marie thought: *nerd stuff?*

The lights dimmed. Hayley went and sat between Marie and Gabby, as if this was a private chat now. "Everyone knows Sterling Vance has always loved

144

music," she said. "They say he's got a guitar collection taking up an entire floor of his house! Girls, I want to know all about his new record label, and all the gossip you've picked up about the music scene!"

Marie blinked. "Um. Well . . ."

"What's it like being friends with Callie Sunny?" Hayley prompted. She looked to her left and right, clearly hoping one of them would say *something*.

All four of the girls floundered for words. Eventually Marie burst out, "She's really sweet. Just like any other friend."

Hayley simpered. "What a kind thing to say. Now, everyone knows that Callie is very secretive about her personal life. I wouldn't ask you to betray a confidence, but what can you tell us about the real Callie?"

"No comment," Marie said.

Hayley gave a flat laugh. "Come on. Surely there must

be *something* you can share with our viewers."

Marie sat in silence. Over to one side, Jeff was waving his arms frantically and mouthing *for God's sake talk!*

Marie looked directly into the camera. The lights dazzled her eyes. She said, "We came here to talk about science. So I just wanted to say to anyone out there who's thinking of studying it, it's worth it. Don't be put off, no matter what anyone says. We need you."

Hallie changed her tone. She became serious and slightly menacing. "That's very true," she said, "because you four haven't had an easy time at all, have you? I know Gabriella lost her brother when she was very young, and Marie, your mum is very ill, isn't she? Is it hard living with someone who needs constant care?"

Marie felt sweat tricking down the back of her neck. The lights burned. She felt panic rising up inside her like milk boiling over. She flashed back to that Camilla

woman sneering down at her the day before. She swallowed hard. Her mouth was dry. She had to say something. She didn't want to.

"I . . . I . . ." Marie stuttered.

"She calls you Marie Curious, doesn't she? Your mum. After that scientist Marie Curie and your curiosity as a kid," Hayley probed.

"What? How did you kn-know that?"

"I know lots of things about you," said Hayley. "I wouldn't be a very good journalist if I didn't!"

Canned laughed played again as Hayley winked at them. It was all too much for Marie.

Why can't people just leave me alone? Is this going to be my life now – other people constantly judging me, making assumptions? Life was so much less complicated when it was just me and Mum and Dad and Izzy, and my cosy little Inventing Shed. Maybe it would be better if

I'd never been picked to go to Vance Camp!

Without stopping to think, Marie got up. She turned and ran for the exit. Behind her people were shouting, but she didn't once look back.

Chapter Twelve

The London Underground was a comfort to Marie. She always felt better riding the escalators down into the depths of the earth. There was something motherly about it, as if the city was holding you in its arms.

I'm like a fox going to ground, she thought. *This is my burrow.*

She sat on the metal bench with the other girls and looked into the darkness of the tunnel. A gathering blast of warm air, like the breath of a sleeping dragon made from scrap metal and rubber, announced an oncoming train. She realised Gabby was still holding her hand. Funny, she'd completely stopped noticing it. When had

she taken it? An hour ago? More?

She gave Gabby's hand a grateful squeeze and let go. "I'm OK now, I think. Thanks."

"You sure?" Gabby said. "We can do the troll hunt without you, if you want to go home."

"I'm good. I *want* to do this."

The train appeared in a rush of sound and lights. A disembodied voice told them to mind the gap. Everyone climbed aboard, took a seat, and braced themselves for what was going to come next.

After everyone had bailed on Hayley's show, they had sat in a café to let Marie calm down and then agreed to focus on finding Callie. As Elisha pointed out, they'd done what Vance wanted. They'd kept their appointment. If

Hayley hadn't got what she wanted out of them, that was her problem. And if Vance was angry, that was his.

"I hope nobody I know was watching," Sophie had sighed. "I'm a scientist. This isn't what I signed up for."

Gabby had provided a welcome change of subject. She'd pinpointed Twinkle's address. Using the data from the comments left on Callie's Instagram and a program of her own devising called Trollbuster, she'd narrowed it down to a housing estate in Islington.

"Calverston Close?" Marie had said. "I've heard of it. It's a rough neighbourhood."

Now, as they rode the clattering underground train through the dark, the mood was tense. Quentin Crump had been creepy, but not nearly as dangerous as they'd expected. Whoever 'Twinkle' was, they had to be a deeply nasty person.

Marie knew some internet trolls could be little more

than jokers, while others just liked to be annoying. But there was also the kind that enjoyed scaring people and making them feel bad about themselves, and Twinkle was clearly one of those.

Trying to take everyone's minds off it, Marie told them all about how Isambard Kingdom Brunel and his father Marc had tunnelled under the River Thames. "Marc invented a special shield to keep the tunnel from collapsing on the workers' heads," she explained. "Can you imagine nobody thinking of that before? And now we've got a tunnel under the English Channel!"

"I wish we could invent an anti-troll weapon," Elisha said.

Oh well, Marie thought, *I did my best.*

"I wish we all had 'stingers' like Rosa's," said Gabby. "They'd be good for self defence."

That reminded Marie of Callie's hotel room the night

she had disappeared. Right from the start something had been wrong, but she couldn't put her finger on it. It was a tiny little detail, something you could easily miss. It nagged at her, like having a word on the tip of your tongue.

The train slowly came to a halt, but there was still blackness outside.

The driver's voice came over the tannoy. "Sorry for the inconvenience, ladies and gentlemen. We're just waiting at a red light. Shouldn't be too much longer now."

All along the tube train, passengers groaned in annoyance. But not Marie. She sat bolt upright and yelled, "Eureka!"

"Er, are you OK?" whispered Gabby. "People are staring at you."

"That was what was wrong! The light was red!" Marie

told her excitedly.

"Yeah," Gabby said slowly, "that's why the train's not moving, we all heard the man."

"No, the light on Rosa's stinger," said Marie. "Remember when Rosa first showed it to us? The light on the side was blue. But when she was lying unconscious on the floor, the light was red and blinking! What could that mean?"

"Well . . . blue lights often mean something's charged, and blinking red usually means out of charge," said Elisha.

"So Rosa's stun gun must have been fired," said Sophie. "Oh, hold on a second. That doesn't make any sense."

"It doesn't add up," Elisha agreed. "Because if Rosa stunned someone . . ."

". . . then where was that person?" Marie finished. "There was only one stunned person there. Rosa."

Gabby said, "Maybe someone forced her own stinger out of her hands and shocked her with it? Someone even stronger and scarier than her."

But before they could talk about who or what could have done that, the train started moving again. Minutes later, they were climbing up the station steps and heading out into the streets of Islington. Like warriors in a fantasy tale, they had a troll to hunt.

Calverston Close was shaped like a concrete horseshoe. Several floors of flats towered up into the evening sky. Some of the windows had satellite dishes, but some didn't even have glass. They were covered up with steel cladding or wooden boards, or just gaped like empty sockets. A single orange streetlight lit up the scene. Two

shops were still open: an off-licence and a fish and chip shop. All the rest had robust metal shutters rolled down.

The girls crossed a patch of scrawny grass where beer cans lay discarded. Dogs barked from several directions, close and angry. A colourful mural had once filled up one brick wall, but now it was almost impossible to see under layers of graffiti tags.

"Where do we even start?" said Sophie.

Elisha whispered, "I don't mind heading into spooky dungeons when I'm playing computer games, but this place is really scaring me!"

What would Mum say at a time like this? Marie thought. "Just stay calm and keep your heads together. And be polite. This isn't a dungeon, no matter what we might think. It's someone's home," she said.

"Look!" Gabby pointed to the graffiti-covered wall. In among all the other tags was the name TWINKLE,

sprayed in pink aerosol paint. The tagger had added little stars around it.

Like finding a troll's footprint, thought Marie.

"Nice one, Gabby! We're definitely in the right place." She looked up at the derelict flats and wondered if Callie was being held in any of them.

"What do you suppose Vance is doing while we're all out here taking risks?" Sophie asked.

"Maybe he's coming up with the ransom money," Marie suggested. Millions, the lipstick message had read. No doubt there would be a call soon, telling him exactly how much and where to leave it.

Elisha said, "So what do we do now? Start knocking on doors?"

Gabby nudged Marie. "I don't think we'll need to. Girls, I don't want to worry you, but – get ready to run."

Marie saw what Gabby had seen. Just across from

them, at the foot of the housing block, a woman was coming out of her flat.

Under the orange sodium streetlight her skin was the sickly white colour of old yoghurt, her hair dyed blonde with long brown roots showing. Her face had a mean, half-starved look, her arms were slathered with tattoos and her eyes were little dark slits in nests of wrinkles. She sucked on a cigarette and tossed it away.

Marie had never seen a more sinister-looking person. Then she spotted the star tattoos, in a long sweep around the woman's neck. The exact same stars as in the graffiti tag.

"It's got to be her," she said.

She felt like a rabbit trapped in the headlights of an oncoming truck. The woman seemed to radiate spite and hatred. Unlike the sweaty, unfit Quentin Crump, she certainly looked like she could have kidnapped

Callie. Too late, Marie realised she was completely out of her depth.

The woman saw them and bared her brown teeth. "Oi!" she yelled. "You! I see yer! Don't move!"

Before Marie could turn and run, the woman came sprinting across the grass, arms waving, right at her . . .

Chapter Thirteen

As the frightening woman charged towards her, Marie thought: *she'll kill me. I'm no good at fighting. I can't run. So I'll scream. Even if I can't do anything else, I can always scream.*

She took a deep breath and got ready to scream her lungs out – but the woman shot past her and kept on running.

Marie turned around. A stocky young man in a black hoodie was standing behind them, arm outstretched. He was only feet away. He must have silently crept up on them, because none of the girls had heard a thing. His hood was pulled over his face and the string was drawn

tight, so only his eyes and nose were peeping out.

The woman dived in front of him, coming between him and Gabby.

"I know it's you in there, Wayne Garvey!" she snarled. "I could smell Lynx Africa from halfway across the estate! Thought you'd mug these four, did ya?"

"I never," protested a muffled voice from inside the hoodie.

"Don't give me that. I know it was you what took Timmy Wilson's Xbox One down the pawnshop last week. That was his Christmas present! You ought to be ashamed!"

"I didn't do nothing!" Wayne insisted, but he was already backing off.

"You would've, if I hadn't have turned up," the woman said. She jabbed her thumb over her shoulder. "You better hop it, sharpish. Before I get on the blower

161

to your grandmother."

Wayne loped away, flicking a rude gesture as he went.

The woman stood with her hands on her hips, watching him go, then turned to Gabby and blew air out of her puffed cheeks. "What do you think you're doing, walking around out here with that nice laptop under your arm? He'd have had it off you in the blink of an eye!"

"Th-anks," Gabby said, lost for words for once.

"That was really k-kind of you," Marie stammered, stepping in.

The woman cocked her head, sizing them up. Marie got a good look at the star tattoos on her neck. From this close, she could see the name *Twinkle* written underneath in flowing joined-up letters. A sickly chill spread through her stomach.

It didn't make sense. Twinkle was a vicious internet troll, but this woman had just saved them from having Callie's laptop stolen. That would have been a total disaster. Why was she being nice?

"You four look lost," the woman said with a grin.

"We're trying to find a friend," Marie said.

"Are you indeed?" The woman smacked her hands together and rubbed them. "Well, you've found me. Fancy a cup of tea?"

And Marie felt she could hardly refuse . . .

The four girls sat around the table in a kitchen that smelled of bacon and cigarette smoke. Marie felt uneasy. There had been another 'Twinkle' tag right outside the front door. She was in no doubt that this woman was the

163

one they were looking for.

But how are we supposed to bring that up, Marie thought. She couldn't very well ask, "Excuse me, are you a troll?"

Four cups of tea were plonked down in front of them. "'Ere you go," the woman said. "I'm Michelle. We've got a motto here on the Close. Don't start nothing, and there won't be nothing."

She chatted merrily away, asking about the girls and where they were from. Marie felt herself starting to relax. Then she told herself not to be so stupid. Just because she's nice now doesn't mean she's nice all the time.

Something upstairs crashed hard on the floor. Marie jumped. She looked up, and Michelle saw her look.

"Don't mind *her,*" Michelle said.

Marie wondered who she meant. Callie couldn't be

imprisoned upstairs – could she? After the confrontation with Quentin Crump, Marie was wary of jumping to conclusions.

She didn't have to wait long to find out as thumping footsteps came down the stairs and a teenage girl burst into the room. Her hair was tied tightly back with candy-coloured scrunchies, her arms were heavy with bright rubber bracelets and she was chewing something. She glanced at the tea mugs on the table. "Didn't make *me* one, did yer?" she sneered.

"Ain't you meant to be doing your homework, Twinkle?" Michelle said wearily.

"Got expelled, dinn' I?" the girl responded with a sniff.

Marie and the girls traded glances.

Of course, Marie thought. *You don't get your OWN name tattooed on your neck, do you? People get tattoos with the names of their partners, their siblings, their*

parents . . . and their children.

"You're Twinkle," Marie said.

The girl looked at her, still chewing. "Remember this face," she said smugly.

"Don't pay any attention to her, for God's sake," Michelle said. "Thinks she's all that, she does. Expelled twice for bullying and only fifteen."

"Calling your own kid a bully," Twinkle announced to nobody in particular. "That's nice, innit?"

Marie knocked back her tea in one gulp and told herself to be brave. "Michelle? I'm sorry to ask, but . . . has Twinkle ever been in trouble for saying stuff on the internet?"

Twinkle grabbed Marie's shoulder. It hurt. "You *what*?"

Marie gulped and did her best to look into Twinkle's angry eyes as she spoke. "We're looking for a troll. Calls

herself Twinkle. Gets her kicks writing nasty things about people online. Has it in for Callie Sunny, the singer. Is that you?"

Twinkle shrugged. "Might be."

"It's her," Michelle said to Marie, and turned disgustedly to her daughter. "Gawd help me, where did I go wrong with you?"

"Why do you do it?" Sophie asked.

Twinkle shrugged again. "Why not? Keeps me off the streets, doesn't it, Mum?" She let go of Marie, pulled up a chair and sat sprawled in it, looking at the girls and basking in their discomfort.

"She does it for the attention," said Michelle. "And she'll go after anyone. Celebrities. Schoolmates. Even one of her cousins. The worse they react, the more she likes it. I take her phone off her, but it never makes no difference. She finds a way."

"Were you picking on Callie Sunny?" Gabby asked Twinkle.

Twinkle swore. "Who cares! She's famous. She's not even a real person." She stood and sidled up to Michelle. "Mummeee? Can I *pwease* have my phone back now? I promise I'll be good."

Michelle rounded on her. "After this? I ought to chuck it out the window."

"But it's been a *week*, you *cow*!" Twinkle screeched.

"What did you call me? That's it. Get up those stairs to your room!"

Twinkle began to hurl abuse at her mother. She slammed cupboard doors and shouted in her mum's face. Bitter words filled the air.

"We'd better go," Marie said. "Thanks for the tea, Michelle."

All the girls hastily got up and headed outside.

Neither Twinkle nor Michelle paid them any attention. Twinkle was in full flow, and Marie was sure nothing Michelle could say at this point would make any difference. She could still hear Twinkle's screaming voice from halfway across the estate.

Nobody spoke until they reached the bus stop. Marie gasped for breath. "That was ugly."

"I guess we can cross Twinkle off the suspect list," Gabby said.

"Yeah," Marie agreed. "By the sound of it, she hates all sorts of celebrities. It's not just Callie."

Elisha added, "Besides, if she's not had her phone for a whole week, she couldn't have sent the text that upset Callie so much."

"So there's only one person left on our list!" Sophie exploded. "One dangerous, powerful person with a grudge against Callie! Someone remind me why we

aren't investigating her again?"

"You *know* why," said Marie.

"Oh yeah. Because Vance said not to. And *he's* always been trustworthy, hasn't he?"

The double-decker bus arrived, and the girls headed up to the top deck. Marie knew what she had to do. She didn't want to, but that hardly mattered now.

"OK," she said. "Hands up who votes to investigate Phoebe Poison next, no matter what Vance says." Sophie's hand instantly went up.

Elisha looked nervous, glanced at Sophie, and then put her own hand up too.

Marie nodded. She put her hand up. "Gabby?" she prompted.

Gabby had opened up Callie's laptop and was staring at the screen.

Marie nudged her. "Yes or no?"

"Uh, guys, remember that phone finder app?" Gabby said. She pointed at the map of London on the screen. A blinking dot had just appeared on it.

Marie gasped. "Wait, you can't mean—"

Gabby nodded. "Callie just turned her phone on. We've got her exact location. Central London. If we're quick, we can catch her!"

"We'd need a car," Sophie said.

"Leave it to me," said Marie. "I know just who to call..."

Chapter Fourteen

"Target on the move!" Gabby said, hunched over the laptop in the front seat of Uncle Eric's black taxi cab. "Approaching the intersection of Queen Street and Clayburn Road."

Marie said, "You don't have to talk like that, Gabby. We're not in a spy movie."

"Tell that to your uncle! He drives like James Bond!"

"You told me this was urgent," said Eric, changing gear. "You want to get there quickly or not?"

Gabby had a point. Marie's stomach lurched as Uncle Eric took the car screeching around another corner. People yelled from the kerb side and made angry

gestures. Up ahead was a red light. Eric slammed the brakes on with a second to spare and the girls all jolted about.

Eric used to be in the army, and though he was a cab driver now, at times like this his ex-military background was all too obvious. Marie couldn't think of many adults she would have trusted more. When she'd called her uncle and asked for a lift to central London, saying only that it was an emergency and every second counted, he had dropped everything to come and pick them up. He didn't even ask what the problem was; he was just there. Marie would be eternally grateful for that.

Now if he could just get them to Callie's location without killing them all, it would be a bonus . . .

Eric yelled, "Oh for God's sake, man! Move your backside!"

The light had changed to green, but the car in front

of them hadn't started moving yet. Eric blasted his horn and the car seemed to get the message. It began to trundle slowly forwards. Eric rolled his eyes and swerved out, overtook the slow car and pulled back into the lane in one move, all with only one hand on the wheel.

With Gabby tracking Callie's position, Eric driving like a commando on a raid and everyone else told to watch out for speed cameras and police cars, they quickly ate up the miles to their destination. When Gabby announced that Callie's phone had come to a stop in Mayfair, Marie got her to read off the street address and checked it on her phone.

"It's a restaurant," she said. "Billbury's."

Eric whistled. "That place is proper posh. The Queen goes there for her birthday tea!" He sucked air through his teeth. "Can't see you lot getting in."

Marie said, "We've got to get in. I don't understand

what Callie's doing there, but we need to find her."

Eric narrowed his eyes. "Right. I know a short cut. Hang on!"

He performed a U-turn in the middle of the road and drove away amid the blare of car horns. Somewhere in the distance a police siren whooped. Eric directed Gabby to open the glove compartment. "There's a blue disabled badge in there somewhere. It's Dina's. Stick it on the windscreen, would you? We can park anywhere with that."

Marie sat and silently prayed they would make it to their destination in one piece.

"Marie?" said Elisha after a moment. "I didn't want to say this, but . . . just because Callie's phone is there doesn't mean that she is."

"Someone could have taken it off her," Sophie agreed.

With a screech of tyres, Eric pulled up outside

Billbury's. "Whatever it is you're up to, good luck," he said. "I'll keep her ticking over. Marie, you owe me one."

"I owe you a lot more than that!" said Marie, climbing out of the car to the welcome safety of the pavement.

Eric grinned. "You're a good kid, Marie Curious. The whole family's proud of you."

The four girls stood and looked up at Billbury's. It looked more like an exclusive London club than a restaurant. Tall stone columns stood in front of glass windows, revealing a scene of gilded luxury inside. Black-suited waiters moved from table to table, serving people who looked like they had just come from the opera or the Houses of Parliament.

Just inside the main entrance, a man stood beside a book on a stand. With his thinning hair, narrow face and pencil moustache, Marie thought he looked like the original English butler that all the other butlers you see

in movies must have been cloned from.

"Is she in there, Soph?" she asked.

Sophie checked the laptop. "Less than a hundred yards away, one floor up," she said.

"This is it," said Gabby.

Elisha nodded. "The moment of truth. Let's find out what's really going on."

Marie strode up and pushed open the double glass doors.

The ground floor was a medley of round tables, mirrors in ornate frames, bar areas with hundreds of colourful bottles, and wealthy-looking people in a hubbub of conversation. Marie looked from table to table, trying to catch a glimpse of Callie's blue and white twists. No sign of her. But there was a sweeping flight of steps up to a second floor, with a balcony overlooking the floor below. That was where she must be.

"Up the stairs," she told the others. "Come on."

She rushed forwards, and the man with the reservations book stepped into their path with the effortless grace of a ballet dancer. "Oh no, no, no. Oh dear me, no," he said. "I'm afraid you can't just charge in. This is Billbury's. I have to check your reservations first."

"We don't have reservations," Marie began, "but there's someone here, and we need to see them, it's urgent..."

The man held up a hand. He gave Marie a piercing look.

She suddenly found she couldn't speak. There was something about him that made her feel hopelessly out of place. It was like being told off by a teacher when you did something wrong at school. You wanted to argue back, but you couldn't. All you could do was shuffle your feet, mumble and look away.

178

"Well brought-up young ladies don't disturb people who are having dinner, do they?" the man said softly.

"But—" Marie tried to say.

"You don't want to make a *scene*, do you?"

Marie's cheeks flushed. "It . . . it's just . . ."

"That would be bad-mannered of you, wouldn't it?"

"Well, yes, I suppose, but . . ." She hung her head.

"Good." The man smiled approvingly, sensing Marie was beaten. "I'm going to have to ask you to leave now. I'm sure there won't be any fuss. Thank you so much for your cooperation."

From behind her, Sophie said, "I'm losing the signal!"

It was like a cold splash of water in Marie's face. Who cared about *good manners*? Her friend's life was at stake!

She turned to Gabby. "Stall him," she said, and lunged past the man.

"YO! SEÑOR!" Gabby declared at the top of her

voice. She banged her hand on the book stand. "DON'T YOU KNOW WHO AM I? I'M STERLING VANCE'S APPRENTICE!"

Forks and knives clinked all across the restaurant as people stopped eating. Everyone turned to look. Gabby's voice only got louder. "YOU DON'T WANNA KEEP ME WAITING TOO LONG!"

Marie sprinted between the tables and bounded up the stairs to the upper floor. *Bless Gabby,* she thought. *She's creating a distraction so I can find Callie – and it's working.*

There were tables all around the balcony. The people sitting at them were looking down on to the main floor, watching Gabby's drama unfold and muttering to one another. None of them were Callie. Over to the side, the kitchen door was swinging back and forth as if someone had just barged through it.

Then Marie saw an empty table. There were two half-finished plates of food. One of the chairs had toppled over. The other had a jacket over the back. It was Callie's size and style. Had she been here? Did something scare her off?

Marie moved closer. The jacket had a bulge in the pocket. A phone. Marie could see the top edge. It glittered with blue gems.

"Security!" yelled the man at the front door. "Get these hooligans out of here!"

Marie had to make a decision fast. She grabbed Callie's phone. But where could Callie herself have gone? Too late, she realised – the kitchen door!

Marie started towards it, but the security guards appeared at the top of the stairs. Before she could do anything more, the four girls were ushered out on to the street and told never to come back.

"Someone was there, and they had Callie's phone, but they ran away," Marie told the others. "But I got the phone."

"So check it already!" Sophie urged.

Marie tried. But, of course, it was locked and needed a pass code.

She sighed. "Let's get home and get some sleep. Today's been insane."

As they walked away, some instinct made Marie turn around and glance back up the street. A dangerous-looking figure was standing in the shadows opposite Billbury's, watching them go. Even at this distance, Marie could tell who it was.

"Rosa," she whispered.

Had the body guard followed Callie's trail this far, too?

Chapter Fifteen

Marie woke up, thinking: *This is the last day. The concert's tomorrow night.*

The first thing she saw was Callie's phone, glittering by the pillow where it had been all night. She picked it up and held it tightly, wishing she could contact Callie telepathically and ask her where she was, and if she was OK.

Vance must be going crazy. Marie wondered if he'd had the ransom demand yet. Maybe it would be better just to pay it, get Callie back and let the concert go ahead. He would lose a fortune either way.

One day left to rescue a rock star, Marie thought

as she cleaned her teeth. *We were so close yesterday.*
We've got to keep trying.

After breakfast, Marie's mum left in a taxi to visit a
friend, and the girls gathered in the Inventing Shed to
go over the clues one more time. Gabby tried to unlock
Callie's phone, but a warning notice flashed up. "Only
two more attempts and if we still get it wrong, we'll be
locked out," she said. "I can't risk hacking it. We need the
code."

"Six digits," Elisha said, looking over Gabby's shoulder.
"I'd guess it's a date. Something that means a lot to Callie."

"Why would Callie leave her phone behind?" Sophie
wondered.

"If she was even there at all," said Marie. "But whoever
had it ran off in a hurry. They probably just forgot."

"Looks to me like we're back to where we were last
night when you called the vote," Gabby said. "And I vote

yes. We've got to go talk to Phoebe Poison, no matter what Vance said about steering clear of her. So what's our next move?"

"We're all scientists," said Marie. "Let's see if we can come up with a theory that proves what we know so far."

"Phoebe was jealous and angry because of Callie's success. She felt disrespected that she came to London, and so she's had someone kidnap her," said Elisha.

"It's pretty crazy," Marie said, "but it does fit the facts."

"Maybe she meant it as a prank at first and it all went too far," Sophie said with a shrug.

Everyone agreed that they had to confront Phoebe face to face. "But how do we get close to her?" Gabby objected. "She's surrounded by security 24/7!"

Marie clapped her hands briskly. "We need to do more research. Everyone, fire up the search engines. Dig

up whatever you can on Phoebe Poison. There's bound to be a crack in her armour somewhere!"

Silence fell, broken only by the sound of Izzy purring on Marie's lap, and fingers urgently typing on keyboards.

It was Sophie who finally said, "Aha! She's playing a concert *tonight*!"

"How are we going to confront her at a concert?" Elisha said, sounding sceptical. "Won't it be a bit noisy?"

"I've got an idea," Marie said. "Listen to this: 'Phoebe's backstage parties are notorious. Not only are they lavish and outrageous, they're where to hear the freshest, most scandalous gossip!'"

"They won't let us backstage without passes," Elisha said.

"Oh, I know," Marie said. "I was hoping our very own computer expert might be able to make some for us!"

Gabby leaned back in her chair and grinned widely.

"Forging passes, you say? Girl, I forged a letter from my mom to get me out of gym when I was six, and I've never looked back! I'm going to need a printer, a laminator and some recent photos of you all. Now, stand back and give me some room. I've got work to do!"

By the time evening rolled around, the backstage passes were ready. All four of the girls had new identities as apprentice music journalists.

"This is amazing work, Gabby," said Marie.

Gabby waved her hand. "Eh, they won't stand close inspection, but they should fool the doormen. Which is all they need to do."

"All we have to do now is get dressed up for a Phoebe Poison party," said Elisha, sounding like she was about to

go and have dental treatment.

Marie wasn't feeling too confident about that, either. "How hard can it be?" she said. "All we have to do is look badass. We've got clothes, accessories, make-up . . . let's just go wild!"

When Marie's mum came home two hours later and saw the result, she wheeled herself to a stop in the middle of the living room and stared.

"Oh, Lord," she said. "Oh, what have you done?" Her mouth quivered as she tried to keep a straight face, but she couldn't hold it in and she let loose a massive cackle of laughter.

Marie stood in a dismal slouch. "Thanks, Mum. Really. Appreciate it."

"This is just like that time when you said you were going to make a birthday cake all by yourself and got covered head to toe in flour and eggs!" her mum howled.

"I was only seven," Marie muttered to her friends.

"Badass, did you say?" sighed Sophie. "I don't know about the 'bad' part, but we've definitely managed to look like ass."

There was no way around it. The four of them looked dreadful. Marie, dressed in a carefully ripped T-shirt and jeans, had tried to draw tattoos on herself in magic marker. Elisha's light pink hijab did not go well with a black studded collar and transparent plastic raincoat. Gabby had overdone the lipstick and had backcombed and sprayed her hair so much that it stuck out in all directions like a fright wig. Poor Sophie had shaved her eyebrows entirely off and drawn them back on. Now she looked like a permanently startled elf.

"Should we take a picture for Instagram?" Marie asked.

"Don't," said Gabby. "It'd crack the phone camera."

Sophie sat down hard on the sofa and groaned. "Why did we think we could do this? We're way out of our league!"

Marie's mum wiped her eyes and chuckled. "OK, enough talking yourselves down. Marie, make some tea and let's get this fixed. You all look pretty mashed-up, I won't lie, but I've seen worse."

Steadily, patiently, Dina helped the girls get ready – properly this time.

She combed Gabby's hair through and tied it up on the top of her head, Arianna Grande style. Then they picked out new clothes together. By the time Gabby was fully kitted out in a white crop-top, denim jacket and tight jeans, along with toned-down make-up, she looked

like she could front a band of her own.

Sophie was next. Dina showed her how to recreate her eyebrows with a kohl pencil, then directed her to her own wardrobe to get dressed up in some retro fashion. She eventually came back through the door full of smiles in a flowing dress and flower crown that wouldn't have looked out of place at Glastonbury.

When it was Elisha's turn, Dina made sure everything was colour-coordinated. A classic little blue dress went brilliantly with a pink silk headscarf, tied loosely behind Elisha's ears so that she could show her dazzling diamond studs. Elisha wanted the make-up kept to a minimum, so Dina gave her a simple dab of blush and some clear lip gloss. Gold bangles completed the look: Elisha looked like she could be a film star.

As for Marie, all she needed was a wardrobe change and a quick shower to rinse off the 'tattoos'. Again, it was

Dina's clothing collection that came to the rescue. Marie thought she'd seen all her mum's old clothes, but some of the stuff that was coming to light now made her eyes pop.

"Mum, were you in the Sugababes or something?"

"Of course not!" Dina laughed. "I was in one of their videos once, though. Just behind Keisha's head."

Marie looked at her reflection in the hall mirror. Dressed in a long black leather trench coat, silk blouse and black skirt, with a belt of silver studs gleaming, she looked like a vampire hunter from the future.

"Almost perfect. Just needs one more thing," Gabby said, and passed Marie a pair of wrap-around sunglasses. Marie put them on and gasped when she saw how cool she looked. *Is that really me?*

The four of them lined up together, and this time Dina did take a photo. "You don't just look like four friends

192

any more," she said. "What you've got here is a *squad*."

Outside, in the street, a taxi beeped its horn.

Marie bent down and kissed her mum on the cheek. "You're the best mum in the world. I don't know what I'd do without you."

Dina squeezed her hand. "Just come back to me safe and sound, Marie."

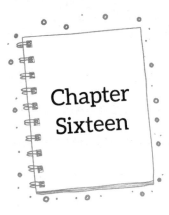

Chapter Sixteen

A thumping bassline pounded out from the rooms behind the stage. Through the smoky darkness beyond, Marie could see people dancing, lounging and glowering at one another. It looked like backstage at the Oscars.

The two men standing on either side of the door were bald, beefy and so alike, they might have been brothers. Marie knew they were going to turn her away. Now she could see what the backstage party was like, she felt relieved she wasn't going to have to go in there after all.

She held up her forged pass, her heart thumping so hard in her ears it drowned out the bass. The nearest doorman barely glanced at it. "In y'go," he said, with the

merest tilt of his head.

And Marie had no choice but to keep walking, through the door and into the thudding beat.

She walked past the gang of girls pouring frozen slushies from a machine, past the boys angrily talking about going outside for a fight, and past the tall girl in the scarlet neon wig, who watched her with amused eyes while she danced jerkily like a robot. She could feel the other three girls following behind her.

The air tasted weird and electric. This wasn't a party like the last one, full of celebrities and fakery. These people were partying *hard*. Marie could feel the energised vibes in the air.

The only place to sit was next to a table that was already full. Marie headed for it, feeling the burning glares from the crew of four other girls who were sitting there, in fur collars and with contact lenses that shone

in the ultraviolet. In the weird purplish light shining up from under the glass tabletop, they looked like witches or extras from *Sabrina*.

"I get the feeling we're on the wrong side of the tracks here," Gabby whispered.

"I've never felt so out of my depth!" said Elisha.

Marie said, "We have to see this through, for Callie's sake. Look! There's Phoebe Poison!"

The singer was closer than they'd realised. It was hard to see anything in this murk. She sat at a private table on a little platform, with steps leading up to it. On one side of her sat a boy with a dancer's build, dressed in an old-fashioned military jacket and scrolling idly through his phone. On the other side, filming with her phone like always, was Hayley MacKenzie. The table was covered with astonishing food. Marie saw profiteroles, cream cakes and a mountain of little spherical pastries with

strawberry sauce drizzled all over them. A huge silver platter had bowls of chicken and fries at one end and sushi at the other. There was even a chocolate fountain.

Phoebe Poison herself was tall and slender, with sweeping eyeliner wings, dark purple lipstick and jet-black hair piled up on top of her head. She wore a blue and white Harajuku-style dress that made the breath catch in Marie's throat. It was almost identical to the ripped-up dress they'd found on Callie's bed!

"Do you see that?" Marie whispered to the girls.

"The plot thickens," said Elisha dramatically. "What's Hayley doing here?"

"Looking for gossip, what else?" Sophie said.

The sight of Hayley made Marie feel like throwing up on the spot. All the panic she'd felt before came back in a churning rush. She sat with her eyes closed, breathing steadily through her nose until she felt calm enough

to go on. Then, moving quickly so she wouldn't have a chance to change her mind, she stood up and walked towards Phoebe. She didn't need to look behind her to see if her friends were following. She knew they'd have her back.

Phoebe didn't even look up. Hayley saw Marie coming and gave her a look of pity that was worse than scorn. The boy leaned over, barring the way between Phoebe and Marie.

"Sorry. You must be at least *this* cool to sit with us," he said in a purring voice and pointed to himself.

"I need to talk to Phoebe," Marie said.

Hayley gave a shrill little laugh and aimed her phone at Marie. "This should be good!"

"What are you poor lost little lambs doing at a party like this?" the boy drawled. "Don't you know what time it is? You ought to be tucked up in bed."

Hayley leaned behind Phoebe and whispered something in the boy's ear. He looked at Marie, pulled a shocked face and then let out a deep throaty laugh.

Marie could guess what sort of thing she'd told him. Hayley knew all about her life, after all.

Sophie tugged at Marie's arm. "Maybe we'd better go," she said.

But Marie stood her ground. "I'm not going anywhere."

Phoebe darted her gaze at the boy. "Jason," she said irritably. "Deal with this."

Jason stretched like a panther and yawned in Marie's face, as if this whole exchange bored him. "Who exactly did your hair tonight, chickie? Was it your *mummy*?" He reached up and pulled the end of one of Marie's braids.

In an instant, Marie's hand grabbed Jason's wrist. With calm, steady strength she pushed him back and down out of her way. His face registered astonishment

at first, then crumpled into despair.

"Don't do that again," she said, "or you'll be crying for *your* mummy. You get me?" She snapped her fingers in Phoebe's face. "You. We need to talk."

Phoebe finally turned to look at her. She had cold, green eyes that made Marie think of snakes. "What? You looking for an autograph?"

"Callie Sunny. Tell me everything you know."

Phoebe laughed. "What's to tell? The girl's fake. A total sellout! She's obsessed with me, you know? Copying my style. If I hadn't called her out, I bet nobody would have even heard of her!"

"She's a better singer than you are, and you know what? She's a better person, too!" Marie yelled.

"Oh, she's sent her fans to throw down with me, is that it?" Phoebe spat.

"I guess she's just too chicken to face you herself,"

Jason said and giggled.

"Chicken?" Marie fumed. "You want chicken? Have some!" Without pausing to think, she grabbed the food platter and flung the entire contents at Jason. But to her horror, he ducked and Phoebe caught the whole tray full in the face.

Marie would remember that sight for a very, very long time. Phoebe Poison standing in front of her, covered in greasy chicken fragments, her face twisted in shock and fury like a half-melted waxwork, with soy sauce dribbling down her front and a creamy profiterole slowly oozing down the side of her head. Her lips wobbled and her throat pulsed as if the scream she needed to utter was just too big to come out.

But it came anyway.

The music stopped. Phoebe glared balefully at Marie, grabbed the profiterole off her shoulder and flung it.

Marie dodged and the profiterole hit someone at the next table with a wet splash.

Howling like a banshee, Phoebe grabbed two more fistfuls of profiteroles and began to pelt Marie with them as if they were snowballs. Creamy gobbets spattered her black leather coat.

"Call security!" Jason bleated. "Someone, have them thrown out!"

"Oh, shut up," said Elisha and tipped a cream cake into his lap.

As the two enormous doormen came striding over, Marie caught a glimpse of Hayley MacKenzie, who was filming every moment of the chaos. She looked happier than a child on Christmas morning.

And then a heavy hand clamped down on Marie's shoulder and a voice was saying "Out!"

Chapter Seventeen

Marie sat on the park swing, scuffing her heels on the ground. The sky overhead was the colour of soggy newspaper. The swing chains creaked. Any moment now it would start to rain. She didn't care.

Back at the house, the girls would be keeping her mum company. They'd be putting a brave face on things. But Marie, who didn't feel up to being brave right now, had gone out for a walk. The park around the corner from her house was a good place for her to go when she was feeling sad. She imagined her dad's hands pushing her on the swing and wished he could be here to push her now, like he used to.

It was the morning of the day of the concert and Callie Sunny was still missing. They'd failed. It was as simple as that.

Marie had woken up to find a voicemail on her phone from Vance. She knew what it was going to say before she even played it. Their throwdown with Phoebe was all over the internet, thanks to Hayley MacKenzie. It was even in the morning papers. She had well and truly got her revenge on the girls for ditching her show.

Marie had put Vance's message on speaker so they could all hear it together. He was absolutely furious.

"You were supposed to make the Solid Sterling record label look good, not drag it into the mud! Sure, rock stars can have some pretty wild parties and trash the odd hotel room, but you aren't rock stars. This is no way for my apprentices to behave. I'm going to have to think seriously about whether to keep the four of you on ..."

They had sat in silence for a long time after Vance's rant had finished.

"Well, it was nice while it lasted," Sophie had said with a sigh. "I guess I'll be heading back to Australia soon. Back to normal life. At least I'll have more time for activism. There's plenty going on back home that I need to kick up a stink about. How about you?"

"Study. Watch football on the big telly with my family. But we'll all stay in touch, right?" Elisha had said.

"Of course. We'll stay friends no matter what!"

"It's all Vance's fault," Gabby had sniffed. "If he'd just paid the money like he was meant to, Callie would've been let go by now!"

Marie swung morosely back and forth. *Funny,* she thought. *Just the other day I was thinking about how it might be better if I'd never been selected for Vance camp. Now it looks like we all might lose Vance as a*

mentor. I can't stop thinking how much I'm going to miss this life.

She leaned her head back and stared up into the grey vault of the sky. "Oh, Callie, where the heck *are* you?" she yelled in frustration.

Her only answer was a few damp drops of rain, spit-spotting on her face.

She should call Vance, she realised. They hadn't found Callie and they weren't going to, so she should tell him to cancel the concert. At least if he cancelled it now, people wouldn't find out at the last minute. He'd have to refund the cost of the tickets, and all the money he'd spent on promotion would be wasted. Not to mention what Camilla would do. But it was the right thing to do.

Marie slipped her phone out of her pocket, found Vance's contact details and braced herself to make the call. Raindrops dotted her phone screen, lying there like

tiny jewels of colour.

It's crazy, Marie thought. *This phone is thousands of times more powerful than the computers on board the spacecraft that took humans to the moon. It's connected to a worldwide net of information. Back in the sixties, it would have seemed like science fiction. And yet I can't even use it to find one missing girl.*

Maybe I just haven't tried hard enough.

On impulse, Marie closed her contacts and opened up YouTube on her phone instead. She searched for "Callie Sunny" and selected the most recent videos. Maybe someone had seen her. At this stage, anything was worth a try.

But the videos that popped up were just the usual, humdrum stuff. *Me and my cousin singing Callie on the ukulele. Is Callie Sunny really a robot? London busker sings Callie Sunny – amazing voice! My Friends Call Me*

Medusa animatic – work in progress – don't hate.

Marie clicked on the busker video. Someone had recorded a young man with long straggly hair and a moustache, playing a guitar. He was singing into a portable microphone on a stand. The quality wasn't very good, but he did have an excellent voice. Marie watched him cover *Stringing Daisies* and then start singing *Blue Summer Skies,* the song Callie had sung at her private concert in the Executive Lounge.

More raindrops landed on the phone. Marie wiped them off, leaving rainbow trails. It was definitely the same song, but the words were different. It wasn't an upbeat love song any more. This song was more bittersweet, about missing someone.

"Hang on a moment," Marie said, and felt a chill that had nothing to do with the rain. "This song was only announced three days ago, at a private gig. So how does

he know it?"

In the video, the busker noticed he was being recorded. Immediately he stopped singing, switched off his microphone and began to pack up his guitar.

Marie's mind swirled with new questions. Was the young man Callie's boyfriend? He must know her, or how could he possibly know the song?

Maybe Marie could find him. She skipped back through the video to the first moments, when the street sign was briefly in view. And there it was – Palmerston Avenue! Buskers often came back to the same spots. If she went there, maybe she could find the busker and find out what he knew.

She sent a link to the video to Gabby, Elisha and Sophie on WhatsApp. Feeling a faint glimmer of hope, she hopped off the swing and began to walk home. And then her phone pinged.

She had a direct message on Insta, from someone called @Your_Auntie_Dote. Marie didn't recognise the name. It read:

Need to talk. Meet me at the British Museum café, twelve noon. Bring your crew but no journalists. I promise it'll be worth it.

"What if it's a trap?" she said aloud to herself.

I have to go ahead with it, trap or not. There are no other leads to go on, and right now, I've got nothing to lose...

Marie looked through glass at the Benin Bronzes, thinking of the people they had been stolen from. There was no sign of her mysterious Insta messenger yet, so Marie had gone for a wander around the British

Museum exhibits. Some of them were fascinating, some enthralling and some just made you angry. Meanwhile, Elisha and Sophie watched from a nearby bench in hastily thrown-together disguises. Sunglasses for Elisha and an old cap of Dina's for Sophie. Gabby had stayed in Marie's Inventing Shed to keep working on the identity of the busker.

A tall dark-haired girl wearing sunglasses came strolling over and stood next to Marie. They looked together at a bronze mask.

"Glad you could make it," the girl said.

Marie looked at her, puzzled.

The girl lowered her sunglasses, revealing green eyes, and winked.

Marie gawped at her. "*Phoebe Poison?*"

"Shush!" Phoebe said and took her arm. "I'm in incognito mode. Let's grab a seat in that corner. How are

you doing, Marie?"

The pair of them sat down. Members of the public strolled back and forth, oblivious to a celebrity's presence. Marie was sure she could feel the world spinning beneath her feet. It was making her feel giddy.

"To be honest, I'm confused," she said. "Why are you being so nice?"

"Oh, you mean last night?" Phoebe chuckled. "That was fun! I'm just sorry I didn't know who you guys were. I've seen the Hayley vids now, and I'm all caught up. Sterling Vance's apprentices!"

Your Auntie Dote, Marie thought. *Your antidote. The opposite of poison. I should have guessed.*

"I just want to know one thing, if you don't mind," said Phoebe.

"What's that?"

"Why didn't you tell me you guys were working for

Vance too? Our food fight was pretty awesome – it even made the papers, great publicity! But if I'd known you all were coming, I could have prepared something even more special!"

"Wait. What do you mean, 'working for Vance too'?"

Phoebe shuffled up closer. "It's meant to be a secret for now, but Sterling Vance is buying my contract out from the label I'm with. I'm joining Solid Sterling! Can you believe it?"

Marie's mind flashed back to Vance warning her not to investigate Phoebe Poison. "Oh, yes," she said softly. "I can believe it all right."

"So when you guys showed up and we had that big fight, I figured that was all part of the publicity," Phoebe went on. "You know, like the Callie Sunny beef. Stuff to keep me and her in the headlines."

"Wait. Slow down." Marie's head was starting to ache.

"Are you telling me that whole falling-out you had with Callie was a *publicity stunt?*"

"Well, sure!" Phoebe's eyes were wide and strangely innocent.

"And that was Vance's idea too?"

"You got it. He paid top dollar for it, too," Phoebe said. "Oh, honey, I'm sorry. Is this all too much? Honestly, that thing with Callie, it wasn't personal. It happens all the time in the music biz. It's just like professional wrestling, y'know? Fake fights. Fall out one week, make up the next. And the public love it. They eat it up."

When I see Sterling Vance next, thought Marie, *I am going to make him wish he was never born.*

"So you don't know where Callie is?" Marie asked.

Phoebe looked blank. "Huh?"

"She's disappeared. She's been missing for three days now. Maybe even kidnapped."

"What? Are you *serious*?" Phoebe seemed genuinely horrified. "Marie, I swear, hand on heart, I didn't know anything about that!"

Marie looked right into her eyes. Phoebe didn't flinch or look away. Marie was sure, then, that she was telling the truth. Whatever else might be fake about Phoebe's behaviour, this was the real her.

Marie's phone rang. "I hope this is Vance," she said, reaching for it, "Because I've got a lot to say to him"

But the caller ID said Gabby.

"Marie?" Gabby said. "You need to get back home. Right away."

"Why? What's up?"

"The busker in that video," Gabby said. "I've found out who it is. Absolutely one hundred per cent certain. And it changes *everything*."

Marie turned to Phoebe. "I've got to go. There's a new

215

clue to follow. Thanks for all your help Phoebe."

"It's OK. I'm sorry again, Marie. Just DM if you need any more help."

Chapter Eighteen

Marie, Elisha and Sophie had rushed back to Marie's house. Gabby met them at the front door, laptop in hand. The video of the busker was on the screen, paused.

Gabby pointed. "See this microphone the busker's using? I checked the details. It's got an autotune feature that lets you change the pitch. You can turn it up high and make it sound like you're a hamster, or – if you're a girl – you can turn it down low and sound like a man."

"Right," said Elisha. "I've heard some girl gamers use that kind of thing online, so people don't know they're female."

"This is what happens when you strip away the

autotune. Are you ready?"

Gabby pressed a key, and they all heard the singer's real voice through the speakers.

"That's Callie!" said Marie.

And she took another look at the busker. The long straggly hair that was clearly a wig – just like the wig they'd found in Callie's hotel room. The moustache, which was stuck on. Once again, Callie's talent for changing her appearance had worked its magic.

"Yeesh," said Sophie.

"OK. Let's put this all together," said Marie. "This video was posted online three days ago, so before Callie disappeared. Why was she out in the London streets, pretending to be a busker, singing a different version of her song?"

Elisha shook her head. "Why would she need to go busking? She's an international popstar. She can put on

a concert to her fans any time. Unless she doesn't care about putting on a big show."

That rang true to Marie. "Maybe that's it. Maybe it's about being *real*. Guys, do you remember when Callie played the song to us? How it sounded . . . well, kind of fake?"

"Yes!" Gabby chimed in. "It was so different from the stuff she'd done before. All happy and smiley, but you could tell she didn't really mean it."

Marie could feel the truth was tantalisingly close, like a stranger outside the door waiting for the right moment to knock. She clenched her fist. She *would* get to the bottom of this.

"If this is about being real, maybe this isn't just a different version of *Blue Summer Skies*. Maybe it's the real version. Does that make sense?"

Gabby set the video back to the start, and they

listened to the song again. Marie paid careful attention to the lyrics.

Blue summer skies can't get through to me.

No one understands what they do to me.

Trails across the sky won't bring you to me again.

Emptiness and broken homes and memories.

Kissed me better when I fell and grazed my knees.

No more kites and bubbles no more climbing trees.

Just pain . . .

In that moment, Marie felt closer to Callie than ever before. This wasn't a mushy song about missing some stupid summer boyfriend. This was about a feeling Marie knew only too well.

"This is a song about wanting one of your parents back," she said.

Sophie added, "But we know her mum's still around. She's her brand manager."

"So the song has to be about her dad!" Elisha finished.

Broken homes and memories, Marie thought. She checked Callie's Wiki page to see if there was anything in there about a family break-up. Sure enough, there was.

"That's it!" she said. "Her father Byron left home when she was only eleven. His relationship with her mother Camilla fell apart, it says."

Marie tried to imagine what that must have been like for Callie. She missed her own dad terribly, but she knew he'd be home again one day, and until then there was always Facetime. What's more, he still loved her mum very much. Callie didn't have that comfort. Marie's heart ached for her.

Gabby folded her laptop shut. "Guys, I hate to say it, but no matter how interesting this all is, it isn't getting us any closer to finding Callie. There's just too much

stuff that we don't know."

Marie reached into her pocket and clutched Callie's phone. She gripped it tightly and imagined she was holding Callie's hand, leading her to safety. *Stay with me. Just a moment longer. We'll figure this out.*

She took the phone out and looked at the infuriating lock screen. Six digits were all that stood between her and the truth. What was it Elisha had said?

Marie frowned in thought. "Hey, can one of you check and see if Callie's dad's birthday is anywhere online?"

"Sure," said Sophie. After a moment, she said, "Byron Sunny, lawyer, place of residence Missouri, date of birth 9th of March 1979."

Holding her breath, Marie typed 090379 into Callie's phone. It buzzed. *Incorrect passcode entered. One attempt remaining.*

Marie felt close to tears. "Oh, no! I was so sure that

would be right!"

"Wait," said Gabby. "What exactly did you put?"

"Zero nine, zero three, seven nine!"

"Are you sure that's what Callie would have done?"

Marie gasped and rolled her eyes. "Oh, man. I'm an idiot. Thanks, Gabby!"

"Huh?" Sophie said. "I don't get it."

As Marie typed their last attempt into Callie's phone, Gabby explained. "Callie's American, remember. We put the month *first* and the day *second*."

A soft *click*. Marie braced herself for another buzz.

But instead, Callie's phone sprang to life. The lock screen vanished and icons appeared. She saw unread messages, missed calls, all the apps Callie had used.

She cried, "Oh my God, we're in!"

Marie sat on the sofa and the others crowded around her, jostling for a look. Marie began to check through

Callie's social media accounts. She was hoping for a clue to Callie's whereabouts, but she never expected to find anything like the secrets she uncovered.

It was half an hour later, with only two hours to go until the concert, and everyone was still shell-shocked.

"I can't believe it," Sophie kept saying. "It doesn't seem real."

"We know it's real. We've got the phone the messages were sent from, right here," said Marie.

"Even so," said Elisha. "You've got to admit, it's messed up."

It was messed up all right. Not all of the nasty messages Callie had been sent had come from the same person. Some had been from Twinkle, some from

224

random trolls. But dozens of the hateful comments had come from one source – Callie herself.

"She called herself a fake so many times over it's like she was punishing herself," said Gabby.

But why would she punish herself? thought Marie. *As if she'd done something she was ashamed of. I wonder . . .*

"I need to check one more thing," she said, reaching for the phone again. "I could be wrong, but if I'm right, it's the key to this whole mystery."

"What are you looking for?" asked Elisha.

"Just before Rosa came and dragged Callie off, someone sent her a text," Marie said. "Whatever it was, it made Callie cry. If she hasn't deleted it, it should still be here . . ."

The girls waited in total silence. Nobody dared to breathe as they watched Marie expectantly.

Marie suddenly slammed the phone down. "That's it. It all makes sense. I know where Callie is." She leapt to her feet and ran to the door.

"Wait!" Gabby yelled, running after her. "Where are you going?"

"Uncle Eric's waiting outside! He can take us to Vance's hotel. There might still be time to fix this!"

"But what did the message say?" yelled Sophie.

"See for yourself!" Marie passed her Callie's phone.

The girls peered closely at it. Finally, they got to see the message that had reduced Callie to tears on the night she disappeared.

It wasn't spiteful or mean or even accusatory. It was a short, simple text. The sender was Rosa Ivanovich, and the message read:

Don't worry. It'll be OK. I've got this.

Chapter Nineteen

Marie sprinted across the hotel foyer, heading for the lifts. Elisha, Sophie and Gabby followed behind her. Marie jabbed the button.

"Are you sure about this?" Gabby asked.

"Phobos One!" said Marie happily.

Gabby frowned. "You aren't making any sense, hon."

"I should have figured it out on the very first night," Marie replied as the lift began to climb floors. "But I made one mistake. Just one. A teeny-tiny one. And it made all the difference! Just like Phobos One."

Elisha said, "Oh, I understand!"

"Well, do you mind sharing with the rest of us?"

Sophie said impatiently.

Elisha explained. "Phobos One was a Mars probe. It cost a fortune. But when they were writing the software to operate it, they missed out one single character. It was only a tiny mistake, but it wrecked everything. The systems went wrong, the batteries drained and the probe was lost."

"Well, go on then, Marie! Tell us what this one mistake was!" Sophie urged her.

Marie didn't answer. She just gave her friends a secretive, confident smile. The lift reached the eighth floor and the doors opened.

"So we're right back where we started. Callie's hotel room," said Gabby.

"This way," Marie said. She strode up the corridor and kept walking until she reached the door to room number 859. She sighed in satisfaction, reached up

and knocked three times.

"But this is Rosa's room. Callie's room was number 858!" said Gabby, sounding more confused than ever.

"Exactly," said Marie. "Callie didn't get to finish the message, remember? Eight five something. When we rushed up here and saw Rosa lying on the floor, we assumed she must have meant 858. In all the excitement, it never even occurred to us that she might have meant 859. And that was the mistake."

The door opened a crack. Marie saw Rosa's face on the other side. "You again?" she growled. "You need to back off! Haven't I warned you enough times?"

"Yes, you have," said Marie. "And we know why. You're protecting Callie like the loyal friend you really are. That's why you agreed to help her fake her disappearance."

"Nice story," Rosa sneered. "Got any proof?"

Marie took a deep breath. "I've got a theory. Ready? You persuaded Callie to zap you with your own stinger. That's why you were unconscious on the floor. The red light on the stun gun showed that it had been used. Callie put the stun gun into your hand to hide the fact that she'd done it. Then she went and let herself into your hotel room with your key card and hid and waited. And she's been hiding there ever since."

"Whooooah," said Gabby.

"Of course, you couldn't keep her in there constantly, because the cleaners would need to come in," Marie went on. "I'm guessing that's why you went out for a meal at Billbury's. We almost caught you there, but you saw us coming from the balcony and ran out through the kitchen, didn't you? You left in such a hurry that Callie forgot her phone. And then you went round the front by yourself and watched us walk away, just to

make sure we'd really gone."

Rosa snorted. "Are you done? Or do I have to listen to any more of this—"

"Rosa, let them in," said a voice from inside the room.

Marie felt as if golden fireworks were going off in her brain. She wanted to shout for joy.

Rosa hung her head, stepped aside and opened the door to let them through.

There was Callie, standing by the window, a sad half-smile on her lips.

Marie ran to her, caught her up in her arms and hugged her for all she was worth. "Oh, thank God, you're safe!" she cried. *"I found you, I found you, I found you!"*

"I'm so sorry, Marie!" Callie sobbed. "I wanted to let you in on it from the start. I tried! But Rosa . . . she was just trying to protect me . . ."

"I know," Marie said. "You tried to signal 859. Because

all this time, you were just in the room next door. If we'd gone there that first night, we'd have found out the truth right away."

Callie wiped away a tear. She looked at the astonished faces surrounding her, and said, "I owe you guys an explanation, don't I? Well, come on in. Get comfortable. And listen to the story of the girl who kidnapped herself."

They sat on the floor in a semicircle while Callie told them the whole story, all the way from the very beginning.

"After Dad left, I started writing songs. It helped me deal with the pain," Callie said. "I didn't much care if anyone listened to them. I just wanted to tell the truth, y'know what I mean?"

Marie nodded. She understood what it was like to miss your dad. "I think that's a big part of what people like about your music. The honesty."

Callie sighed. "Then the Solid Sterling deal came along. Between Vance and my mom, they cooked up this big rebrand. No more weird quirky songs, nothing gloomy, nothing edgy. I'd finally written a song all about my dad, and how much I miss him, and they . . . they made me change it. Because nobody would want to buy the sad version, apparently. And I know you guys said you liked the new version, but I hate it! It's so fake!"

"Sorry, Callie. We didn't actually like it that much," Gabby said.

"Really?" Callie gave a half-laugh, half-sob.

"I guess we all said what we thought you wanted to hear," said Marie. "We should have been honest."

"It's OK. I know you were just being kind. But after

233

that gig, I went and cried my eyes out. I could feel myself slipping away. I was turning into a fake, manufactured thing. The perky pop princess my mom wanted me to be."

"But you couldn't go through with it in the end," Marie said gently.

"I was trapped, Marie!" Fresh tears flowed down Callie's face. "Booked in to do this big concert, with all this new material that Vance and my mom put together. You know who really wrote my new songs? Vance's computers! Artificial intelligence making pop based on freakin' marketing surveys!"

"Wow," said Sophie. "No wonder you went out busking."

"It was my last little taste of freedom," Callie said and sniffed. "And then I had a crazy idea. A way to get out of having to do the concert. Something neither Vance nor

my mom could predict would happen."

"A fake abduction," Gabby said. "Jeez. I faked notes from my mom to get out of gym, but this is on another level!"

Callie said, "Of course, I'd need Rosa's help. I asked her. I begged. And she said no."

"At first. But when I saw how bad Callie was suffering at that party, I knew I had to step in," Rosa said.

It was funny, thought Marie. Rosa, who had seemed so stern and scary, had been Callie's loyal friend throughout this whole mess. "That's why you cried when she sent you that text," Marie told Callie. "You weren't upset, you were relieved. Because she was finally agreeing to help!"

"That rooftop party was horrible," Callie said. "Fake people. Fake niceness. Fake me. And I knew that was going to be my life from that moment on. I had to get

out. And thank goodness Rosa made it happen."

"Why risk it all by going to eat at Billbury's, though?" Sophie asked.

Callie looked out of the window. "My dad," she said. "When I was little, he always used to say that he'd take us to visit London one day. We'd go and see Buckingham Palace and Nelson's Column and have dinner at Billbury's. Because only a place that was good enough for the queen was good enough for his little girl! It was stupid, but I had to go. I wanted to make it come true."

"There's only one thing I don't understand. Why the note on the mirror saying 'this will cost Vance millions'?" said Elisha.

"I was trying to talk myself into going through with the concert after all," Callie said. "I knew if I didn't, it would cost Vance a fortune. So I wrote that message to myself, because I felt like such a bad person. Which I

am. I'm fake and I'm weak and I brought all this on my own head."

Marie went and took both Callie's hands in hers. "Stop that. You're not weak, or fake!"

Callie squeezed Marie's hands, leaned close and whispered, "But what am I meant to do now? My plan's a bust. You've found me. The concert's going to have to go ahead. So tell me, how am I supposed to get up on that stage and pretend to be someone I'm not?"

"You don't," Marie said simply. "You tell the truth instead. And we're going to help you do it." Then she picked up her phone and typed a message to @Your_Auntie_Dote.

Chapter Twenty

The O2 Arena was packed. In row upon row of seats, people sat excitedly waiting for Callie Sunny's first ever live concert. With ten minutes left to go, the atmosphere was sizzling with anticipation. Up on the stage tall speaker stacks stood waiting to blast Callie's music out. Holo-projectors swivelled back and forth, ready to put on a spectacular light show.

Marie and the girls were in a closed-off room just behind the main stage, where the controls and switches were. Video screens showed the eager crowds. They were starting to clap and call out Callie's name.

"Everything loaded up?" Marie asked Gabby.

Gabby looked over from the holo-projector control panel. "All set. We're ready to do this."

Marie checked one screen in particular. It showed Vance and Camilla, sitting in the front row. For once, they both looked pleased. Marie smiled. They had no idea what was coming.

She turned the dial that brought the house lights down. The chanting from the crowd changed to yells and cheers. It was finally happening!

A spotlight shone down, lighting up the stage. But it was Phoebe Poison who walked out into the light. The crowd stopped cheering and began to murmur. Marie saw Vance's expression change from smugness to confusion.

Phoebe gripped the mic stand and said, "Ladies and gentlemen, good evening! I'd like to introduce you to a very good *friend* of mine. That's right, I said a friend."

Her green eyes blazed in the spotlight. "And whatever rubbish I said about her before, I take it back. This girl is braver than you could ever know. She's no fake. Callie, come on out!"

Callie came and joined Phoebe on stage, with a simple acoustic guitar around her neck – the same one she'd gone busking with.

The crowd began to clap politely at the sight of her, though it sounded uncertain. Callie smiled shyly, gave Phoebe a hug and stood by the microphone. Once the applause had died down, she began to speak.

"I'm scared," she said. "And nervous. And despite what Phoebe said, I don't feel very brave right now. But I want to tell you the truth. So please bear with me." She strummed the guitar. "Mom, I'm sorry if it hurts you, but I have to be true to myself. I won't pretend. And Mr Vance? If you want someone to sing songs written by

computers, you can do it yourself. Because that's not who I am, and I won't change for any amount of money."

Marie crossed her fingers hard. *Good luck, Callie*, she thought.

"Ladies and gentlemen, this is *Blue Summer Skies*, and it's about my dad. I hope you like it."

As she began to play the sweet, sad melody, with nothing but her guitar for accompaniment, the holo-displays began to project their images up into the darkness above the stage. They showed photos from Callie's life. Pictures of her when she was young, riding on her father's shoulders. Callie and her father eating ice cream. Callie dressed as a camel for the school nativity play.

Marie felt tears prickling her eyes. She thought of her own dad and wished he could be by her side right now. At the same time, she felt worried for Callie. What if the

audience didn't like the song?

Then she realised this was the first chance the audience had had to see Callie as she really was. She was such a chameleon online, with all her make-up and quirky outfits, that these pictures from her childhood showed who she really was, underneath it all. She wasn't just telling the truth with her song, she was telling it with her whole self.

The audience listened as the song echoed out through the night air. Vance's face was unreadable. This wasn't the sickly pop anthem he'd thought he was getting. *Good*, Marie thought. *It's OK to feel sad. It's not healthy to keep all the negative emotions locked away.*

As Callie finished the song, there was dead silence. She stood facing the audience, awaiting their judgement.

Callie's mother was the first to stand up and begin clapping. More and more people joined in. The whole

stadium was suddenly a roaring storm of applause. Callie grinned modestly and took a little bow. As the cheers and calls of support rang out, Callie's mother came up to the edge of the stage, holding her arms up.

Callie bent down and hugged her.

"Oh, honey," her mother sniffed. "I know it's hard. He'd be so proud of you. Just like I am."

After a long loving hug, Callie went back to the microphone. "Thank you! Now, what do you say we blow the roof off this place?"

The audience howled their approval.

"OK. I'm gonna need some help here. Phoebe, come on back!"

Phoebe Poison came back on to the stage, to even more wild applause. "You and me are going to be like sisters from now on," she said.

"I want you all to welcome some other friends of

mine," said Callie. "Marie, Gabby, Sophie and Elisha! Come on up!"

Marie ran on from backstage with the other three close behind. The crowd cheered and called her name. Marie waved to them.

"This is a snakey little number called *My Friends Call Me Medusa,* and it's about showing people your true self," Callie said. "I think one or two of you might know it. So feel free to sing along."

She snapped her fingers – one, two, three, four – and a sudden thundering power chord announced the beginning of the song. As the beat kicked in, Callie beckoned Phoebe over to share the microphone. She put one arm around Phoebe and the other around Marie. Gabby, Elisha and Sophie joined in on the ends until they formed a chain, all facing the crowd together.

Callie's clear, confident voice rang out once again.

Marie looked up into the dazzling glare of the spotlights, the crowd's roars of applause echoing in her mind, and thought: *You know, I could probably get used to this after all. Who hasn't dreamed of being a rock star?*

Epilogue

Back at the hotel, the after-show party was in full swing. Marie spotted many of the same celebrities as she'd seen at the rooftop party. This time, they all seemed to be talking very earnestly about honesty and telling the truth, and how important it was to show your true self to the world. Marie shook her head and smiled to herself.

She caught sight of Vance leaning against the wall, sipping an enormous blue drink with an umbrella in it. "Marie!" he called. "Nice job! All worked out in the end, huh?"

"Yes, it did," Marie said frostily. "No thanks to you!"

"Aww, what are you mad at me for this time?" Vance drawled and gave her a cheesy grin.

"Phoebe told me everything," Marie said. "How you paid her to start a beef with Callie, all for the sake of publicity."

Vance shrugged. "That's show business, kid. The public don't want the truth. They just want a good story."

"I wonder. Did you bother to warn Callie first? I don't think you did, did you? She had to read all those nasty words Phoebe said about her, and she thought they were real!"

Vance looked smug. He whispered, "You know what makes an act really believable? When the person performing doesn't know it's an act."

Marie stood there, smouldering with anger. He'd promised to change his ways. And now here he was, getting away with this manipulative behaviour again!

But the next second, Vance's face wobbled like a rubber toy. His eyes crossed. His whole body shuddered. He slowly sank to his knees and toppled over face-first on to the floor.

Rosa was standing behind him, holding her stinger in her hand. Marie's mouth fell open. Rosa had just shocked her boss in the back of his neck!

"Consider this my resignation, Mr Vance," she told his crumpled form. She turned to Marie and winked. "It was a lousy job anyway. See you around, Marie."

Marie looked down at Vance's quivering body and stifled a giggle. She stepped carefully over him, wondering idly how angry he'd be when he came round, and headed over to the other end of the room where Callie was talking to her mother.

"I never wanted you to feel like you couldn't be honest about your feelings. I just wanted you to be

happy and successful!" explained Camilla.

"Nobody can be happy all the time, Mom," said Callie. "But I have to say, I'm feeling pretty good right now." She looked at Marie and smiled. "You guys are going to keep in touch, right?"

"Of course!" Marie said.

After all, she thought, the squad already has an inventor, a math's genius, a hacker and a biologist. I'm sure we can find room for a rock star, too . . .

Have you read the first book in the series?

Read on for a sneak peek ...

As soon as she got home from school, Marie Trelawney shrugged off her blazer, hung it up carefully and pulled on a white lab coat. She headed across the back garden of her terraced house towards a shed with KEEP OUT written in luminous paint on the door. With her notebook and a packet of biscuits under her arm, she unlocked the door and let herself into her favourite place in the whole world – her Inventing Shed.

At twelve, Marie was taller than most and looked out on to the world with wide, inquisitive eyes. An almost invisible dusting of freckles lay across the bridge of her nose. Her neat, sable braids hung down to her shoulders. Instead of jewellery she wore three silicone wristbands: one read M.S. AWARENESS, another YOUNG CARERS, and the third had once read OUR PRINCESS in silver letters but the writing had rubbed off long ago.

Unlike most sheds, there were no lawnmowers, rusty wheelbarrows or bikes gathering cobwebs inside. A throw rug covered the floorboards, and strings of fairy lights hung down from the ceiling, lighting the room in shifting rainbow colours. The walls were covered in posters, most of which Marie had made herself. Up at the top was a cartoon of Katherine Johnson, the genius who calculated how the first NASA spaceflight could orbit the earth. Further down there were photographs of Marie's other favourite female scientists, a framed certificate for winning the Huxley College Science Fair and a picture of a pug wearing a lab coat and goggles.

Marie had known she wanted to be an inventor since she was little. Back then, she'd driven her mother crazy by taking household items apart. Like the time when she'd rewired the toaster and almost burned the house down, just so she could find out how it worked.

Her mum had nicknamed her Marie Curious after the French scientist and her curiosity about all things mechanical had only grown stronger over the years. The shelves inside the Inventing Shed were lined with her gadgets and contraptions.

Marie sat down in the enormous, lumpy armchair she'd been given when her neighbour had moved and set her notebook on the workbench. It was a grubby, glorious thing filled with doodles and designs and covered in stains. There were tea stains, oil stains, soup stains and one or two cat paw prints.

"Izzy!" called Marie, helping herself to a biscuit.

A scrappy mog appeared at the half-open window, yawned lazily and squeezed in. Izzy, named after the famous engineer Isambard Kingdom Brunel, paraded back and forth on the workbench, trampling on the pages of Marie's open notebook.

Marie stroked her cat's soft back, enjoying the engine-like rumble of his purr. Apart from her parents, Marie loved nothing more in all the world than her pet cat.

As Izzy batted his head against her hand, Marie grinned and said, "You want to play, don't you?" She reached for a remote control unit and pressed a button on it.

Out from under her workbench shot a robotic mouse with a big dent in his back and one glowing red eye.

"Hi, Ro-DENT!" Marie chuckled. "Feel like giving Izzy some exercise?"

Izzy's pupils grew large. He wiggled his haunches and pounced. Marie laughed and made Ro-DENT dart away from him.

Marie was very fond of the slightly bashed-up robot mouse she'd invented. Not only could he whizz around on powered wheels, he had magnetic paws so he could scurry up metal surfaces like the fridge, and his eye had a laser pointer built in so he could drive Izzy wild chasing the red dot.

Marie raced Ro-DENT back and forth across the rug, making Izzy perform sudden U-turns and nearly sending him careering into the wall. Then, without warning, Izzy stopped in his tracks and stood there with his ears twitching.

"What's wrong, Iz?" Marie asked. "What can you hear?"

A moment later she heard it herself. A strange high-pitched whine was coming from outside – from above. It reminded Marie of the sound her mum's electric wheelchair made when it got jammed on the edge of a kerb.

She ran out into the garden and looked up. Her eyes went even wider than Izzy's had.

Hovering high over her head was a chunky white delivery drone with four huge rotors the size of dustbin lids. It was carrying a parcel.

It won't be for us, Marie thought.

But the drone was already descending. A robotic-sounding voice announced, "Delivery in progress. Please stand back."

The drone touched down lightly on the grass. Marie felt like she was having an alien encounter.

"Mum!" she yelled. "Come and look at this!"

The drone released its package. Then it shot up into the air, much faster than it had landed. Marie shaded her eyes and watched it whizz over the North London rooftops until it was gone.